River's Run:
Lords of Kassis: Book 1

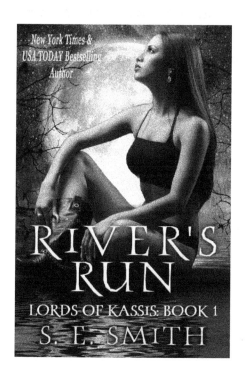

By S.E. Smith

Acknowledgments

I would like to thank my husband Steve for believing in me and being proud enough of me to give me the courage to follow my dream. I would also like to give a special thank-you to my sister and best friend Linda, who not only encouraged me to write but who also read the manuscript. I would also like to thank my dear friends who have supported me: Sally, Lisa, Julie, Chris, and Jackie who have been there through thick and thin.

—S.E. Smith

Montana Publishing
Science Fiction Romance
RIVER'S RUN LORDS OF KASSIS BOOK 1
Copyright © 2010 by Susan E. Smith
First E-Book Publication February 2010
Cover Design by Dara England and Melody Simmons

Summary: River sneaks aboard a spaceship to rescue her two sisters, and makes a deal with a group of alien prisoners who have no intention of following through with their end of the deal.

ISBN: 978-1-942562-58-0 (paperback)
ISBN: 978-1-942562-20-7 (eBook)

Published in the United States by Montana Publishing.

{1. Science Fiction Romance – Fiction. 2. Science Fiction – Fiction. 3. Paranormal – Fiction. 4. Romance – Fiction.}

www.montanapublishinghouse.com

Synopsis

River Knight was looking forward to a peaceful vacation in the mountains with her two best friends, Jo and Star, sisters of the heart. When she travels up into the mountains of North Carolina to the cabin Star has rented for them, she is shocked when she finds the two sisters being abducted. Following them, she discovers their abductors are anything but human.

Sneaking aboard the shuttle in an attempt to rescue them, she finds herself on an unplanned vacation to the stars. In a desperate attempt to save Jo and Star, River makes a deal with a group of other aliens who had also been captured – she'll release them if they promise to return the three girls to their home.

Torak Ja Kel Coradon, Leader of the House of Kassis and next ruler of the Kassis Galaxy, has other plans when he sees the blue-eyed warrior woman. He plans on claiming her for himself and the only home he has plans on her returning to is his.

The three women are believed to be the prophesied warriors sent to join forces to bring peace to the House of Kassis. Worlds collide when the male dominated world meets three circus performers who use their talents to fight for those they love.

When an assassin threatens Torak's life, River has to show him even a circus performer can be a warrior when challenged. The biggest challenge is to Torak's mind as he discovers women from other galaxies are more than they seem.

Can their love overcome the chasm of a few million light years or will an assassin end it all?

Contents

Chapter 1

"I'll be there. It might be late by the time I get there, but I'll be there, I promise," River said, sitting on the bed in the hotel she had just arrived at in California.

"Do you swear, River?" Star asked anxiously.

Star was twirling her shoulder-length blond hair around her finger and looking at her older sister, Jo. She had been trying to get through to River Knight for the past two days. It had been far too long since she had seen her best friend and surrogate sister.

"I swear, Star," River laughed. "And tell Jo she still owes me for the last time we got together."

Star grinned at Jo giving her the thumbs-up sign. They had been trying to get the three of them together for the past year. Now, everything was set. They would finally see each other again.

"She's coming!" Star said excitedly, wrapping her arms around Jo's neck and dancing around.

**

River let out a tired sigh, rolling her shoulders around to ease the tension. She had a lot to do in the next couple of days if she was going to meet up with her two best friends. She grinned.

They were really more like sisters to her. They were her only family now. She had grown up traveling with the circus and had met them when their parents had joined when she was five.

The Strauss Family Flyers were known for their high-wire acts. When Star and Jo's parents retired several years ago, it became the Strauss Flying Sisters. River's parents did just about everything from tightrope walking to the high wire to River's specialty, knife throwing. River had been born into the life of a circus performer just as Jo and Star had been.

They grew up moving from town to town, country to country, nomads in a modern world. The life had actually been very fulfilling. They were very well loved and protected. Their schooling consisted of learning a wide variety of languages as well as learning how to do all types of incredible tricks. They had more parents, grandparents, aunts, and uncles than any girls could ever imagine having. It had hurt when River's parents were killed in a hotel fire during one of their stops when she was seventeen, but her circus family had gathered around her and supported her.

Two years ago, Jo and Star decided they were tired of all the traveling and accepted jobs with Circus of the Stars in Florida. They bought a condo and loved the stability of living in one place. River continued traveling with the circus.

At almost twenty-two, she was the youngest of the three. The circus had just finished a tour in Asia, and she was glad to be home. The girls promised each other they would get together at least once a year.

Last year, Jo convinced River to meet them at their condo where Jo produced at least a dozen different guys for River to meet. River knew what they were up to. They thought if they could get her interested in someone she would settle down. River still enjoyed traveling too much to put down roots. All the guys left her feeling awkward and clumsy, which was ridiculous when one considered she could hit moving targets with a series of knives while gliding through the air upside down held only by her ankles.

River just wasn't comfortable around the opposite sex. She always felt a little different. It might be her appearance. She looked more like an elf.

Oh, not one of Santa's—more like one from the Hobbit. She wasn't really tall at five foot six, but she was very willowy. She had thick dark brown hair that hung to her waist, pale skin, and huge dark-blue eyes outlined by thick dark lashes.

Most people thought she wore colored contacts when they first met her. She usually wore dark sunglasses when she was out because her eyes were so different. She didn't mind when she was performing—it helped with the mystique about her— but out in public she would often be stopped and stared at. Her parents used to tease her, saying she had been a gift from the stars, which she might have believed if her mom hadn't had the same unusual eyes.

River was glad they had decided to meet somewhere else this year. Star had picked out a cabin in the middle of nowhere. They were supposed to meet up in the mountains of North Carolina in two days. River was still in California so she had to make arrangements for a flight.

She called Ricki, who made all the travel plans for the circus, and within an hour she had all her flight arrangements done including her e-ticket and leased car. The joy about Ricki making the arrangements was River didn't have to worry about the usual restrictions for car rentals. Everything went through the company.

Pulling a big, black bag that resembled a duffel bag onto the bed, River opened it to look at her collection of knives carefully packed. She was very, very picky about her knives. They were her life, literally. She had been tossing, juggling, and throwing them since she could walk. Some of the acts her dad taught her had never been performed by anyone else in the world.

She was known as the best of the best when it came to anything involving a blade. While she made sure that everything had survived the shipping from Asia, River couldn't help but laugh at the memory of the reaction of customs official on both sides of the ocean. Ricki had been there to take care of everything, thank God.

Now, River had the next three months off as the circus broke for a much needed rest. She would spend most of it at the cabin Star had rented, practicing new acts. Closing the bag, she finished packing her other belongings before getting ready for bed. She was so looking forward to the peace and quiet of the mountains.

* * *

Everything worked out well. She made the flight and for once she didn't have to produce documentation about her duffel bag. She had gone ahead and checked all her baggage so she wouldn't have to deal with it in the cabin of the plane for the long flight. After she plugged in her iPhone and placed her sunglasses firmly on her head, she was left blissfully alone for almost seven hours.

Picking up her two bags at the airport, she placed them in the trunk of the rented black SUV and began the three-hour drive up into the mountains. She wouldn't get there until after midnight. It was a warm evening, but she couldn't resist driving with the windows down. S

he loved the freedom of the wind blowing through the window. She stopped for gas and a quick bite to eat an hour out as she didn't want Jo or Star to feel like they needed to cook for her so late. She couldn't suppress the thrill of seeing them.

She did miss them so much. No one could separate the three of them during their teenage years. River was two years younger than Star, who was a year younger than Jo. She had always been the one everyone protected the most.

There was a full moon, and the gravel road was lit up as River pulled up toward the cabin. The road for the past ten miles had been winding around and around the mountain. Star told her to park in the garage, which was located below the cabin. She would have to tote her stuff up a narrow path to the cabin.

River found the garage with no problems and pulled in next to Jo's SUV with Florida tags. River grinned when she read the bumper sticker saying "Flyers Do It Better." Grabbing her black duffel bag in one arm and her smaller carrier in her other, she quietly pushed the button to close the trunk. She bent down and pulled one of her smaller knives out of the bag to slide in her boot.

She didn't know what types of animals lived in the mountains, but if she was walking through the woods at night she wanted at least one knife with her for protection. Moving out under the bright moon she was glad she had worn her black jeans and put on her black sweater to ward off the cool mountain air. She would have glowed in any of her other jackets with their rhinestones.

Walking along the moonlit path up to the cabin, River was enjoying the peace and quiet until a scream ripped through the air, followed by a second one. River froze for a moment before she dropped her bags and took off at a run toward the cabin. She skidded to a halt behind a tree when she heard what appeared to be a growl. Reaching down to her boot, she pulled a knife from the sleeve hidden inside it.

Moving up toward the front porch, she jerked back when the door suddenly opened, and a huge figure moved out onto it. She crouched down so she wouldn't be seen. Peeking around the corner, her breath caught in her throat when she realized more than one huge creature was coming out of the cabin. She counted three of them; two of them appeared to be carrying something wrapped in blankets.

River shook with fear as she watched the huge creature turn at the bottom of the stairs. Its face, if you could call it that, was elongated and had what looked like scaly green skin. It turned and hissed at the other two. As they moved down the steps, River almost fainted when she saw Star's arm hanging limply down its back. The creatures started moving down another path on the far side of the cabin.

River slid the knife back in her boot and took off toward the path she had just come from. If she was going to try to save them she needed more than the one knife in her boot. Sliding on the leaves, she grabbed her black duffel bag and took off running after the creatures. She didn't have any idea what she would do when she caught up with them.

River rounded the cabin cautiously before moving down the path on the other side of the cabin. She could hear them moving up ahead of her. She moved silently, keeping as close as she could to the trees so the shadows would help hide her. They moved at a lumbering pace, their long legs taking steps twice the length of hers.

She froze suddenly when one of them stopped and turned around. Keeping her head down so her face wouldn't be as visible, she held her breath. After what seemed like hours, the creature hissed at the one leading them and turned to move down the path again.

River followed them for almost two miles before they came to a clearing. She stood frozen behind a tree as she watched them move into what appeared to be some type of spaceship. It was almost as long as a football field. The two creatures carrying her friends moved up a platform that was opened in the back.

River could see lights shining dimly in the interior. The one leading hissed at the other two as they moved up the ramp, but it remained outside the spaceship. A few minutes later the two creatures returned. A loud noise off to the left side of the ship suddenly caught their attention. All three hissed and took off running toward the woods.

River shook with fear as she moved toward the spaceship, keeping an eye on the woods where the creatures had disappeared. She didn't know if there were any more in the spaceship or not, but she knew she needed to get to her friends and get them out. Pulling her duffel bag straps over her shoulders, she slowly climbed up the ramp, casting quick glances all around her.

Moving up the ramp she saw a narrow corridor leading to a larger opening. Moving swiftly through the corridor she glanced around the interior of the spaceship. In front of her was another corridor that looked like it led to the front of the spaceship. On each side of her there were a series of seats with what appeared to be storage compartments above and below them.

Chained to two of the seats were Jo and Star; both of them were unconscious. River moved toward them with a silent cry. She put her hands on their cheeks and gave a sigh of relief when she felt their warm breath against her palms.

"Jo, Star, wake up. Please, wake up," River called out softly.

She looked at their wrists and noticed they were both chained to a metal bar between the seats. She gripped their wrists to look for where the key went in to see if she could pick it. All three of them were good at picking locks. Marcus the Magnificent, the most famous magician in the world, had shown all three girls how to pick locks before they had learned how to ride a bike. She twisted the cuff on Jo's wrist around and around but didn't see where a key would fit into it. Jo gave a slight groan as River moved the cuff.

"Jo, wake up. It's me, River. Please wake up," River softly said again.

"River?" Jo whispered. Jo's eyes suddenly flew open in horror. "River, you have to run. Run, River. Don't let them get you." Her eyes flew back and forth as she struggled to free herself.

"I can't leave you and Star. We have to get out of here," River whispered back.

"There isn't time," Jo said as her eyes filled with tears. She looked at Star, who was still unconscious. "Oh, Star."

"Come on. You have to help me figure out how to get these off you before they come back," River whispered frantically. She pulled the knife from her boot and tried to pry at the metal.

"Where are we?" Jo asked weakly.

"It looks like some kind of spaceship," River replied softly. "The creatures that had you and Star carried you here. I don't know what they are. What happened?" River asked.

She was trying to keep Jo occupied while she worked on the cuff. There had to be some way to get it off them. If she had more time she knew she could figure it out. There was always a way.

"I don't know. We were waiting up for you. I heard a noise and thought you might need some help, but when I opened the door to the cabin it was to those creatures. I screamed and tried to close the door, but it just ripped it right off the hinges. Star ran for the bedroom, but one of them caught her and she fainted. I don't remember much after that. They put something across my mouth and everything went dark," Jo whispered hoarsely. She began shivering uncontrollably.

"They're coming back! I can hear them. Run, River. Run," Jo began crying softly now.

"Never. I won't leave you," River said, sliding her knife back into her boot.

Looking around, she dropped down to pull open one of the compartments under the seats. It was filled with boxes of some type. Moving down the row, she hurriedly opened and closed them until she found one in the corner that was empty. Removing her duffel bag, she slid down feet first into the compartment, pulling her duffel bag in front of her, then reached over and closed the compartment.

Jo stared at River before nodding. River would not abandon them, ever. Closing her eyes, Jo let the darkness of unconsciousness take her away from the fearful creatures boarding the spaceship.

Chapter 2

River looked out the front of the spaceship she had stowed away on for what seemed like the millionth time. It turned out the spaceship the creatures used on Earth was just a shuttle to a much, much larger ship. Once they docked with the larger ship the creatures carried Jo and Star out. River remained in hiding until she felt sure all the creatures had left the shuttle. Now, she moved about the empty shuttle trying to get familiar with what she had gotten herself into and waiting for the shuttle area to clear out a little.

Peeking out the front view panel, River watched as about ten of the creatures moved containers about. She watched as the one creature who she suspected was the leader of the shuttle crew who had taken Jo and Star argued with another one who was almost twice as big as it was.

The bigger creature hissed loudly and pointed at Jo's and Star's unconscious bodies wrapped tightly in the blankets. The smaller creature hissed something back, then flinched with the other one roared. The other two creatures took a step back and looked like they would have preferred to have been anywhere but there. Finally the huge creature hissed something at the two holding River's friends, and they followed him. The other creature just hissed and left the shuttle bay by another exit.

River knew she needed to find a way around the ship without being seen. These creatures were huge compared to her, Star, and Jo. Looking up, she noticed a series of platforms leading to the ventilation system. If she could get to it unseen, she could move through the vents. The creatures were too large to fit in them. Besides, wasn't that what they did in the movies? If she could stay with them, she could find her friends and they could hide out until they figured out a way to get off the ship.

Satisfied with her plan she just needed to wait until things calmed down a little. In the meantime, she explored the shuttle for any type of food or drinks and a restroom. Finding a box with what appeared to be emergency rations, she stuffed as much as she felt she could safely carry into her duffel bag. She needed to get ready in case she needed to defend herself.

Opening her duffel bag, she pulled out some of the harnesses she used to carry her knives during her performances. She pulled her sweater off placing it in the duffel bag. She might need it later but not while she was climbing.

Pulling on a tight, long-sleeved, form fitting black spandex shirt, she strapped on two of her leather wrist holders which contained seven small knives in each holder. Next, she grabbed her back and chest holder. It criss-crossed her front and back and allowed her to put all types of knives and throwing stars in it, including two small swords which fit in an X-formation on her back. Pulling on her belt, she put additional small throwing stars in it. She used this belt when she was riding bareback and throwing them at candles lit around the ring. She had maybe twenty-five very sharp throwing stars in it.

Lastly, she pulled out several of her favorite throwing knives and placed them in the inserts she had in her leather boots. Closing the duffel bag, she pulled the straps tight so she could run faster if she needed to.

River waited almost two hours before the shuttle area had become deathly quiet. She watched as the last creature left the area, and the lights dimmed. Moving toward the opened ramp which had been left down after their arrival, River stayed as low as possible, moving slowly so she could listen for any noises.

Grabbing the side of the ramp, she flipped under it so she was covered. Peering out, she moved swiftly when she felt confident she was safe toward the nearest stack of cargo boxes, slipping between two of them. She followed the tight corridor between the crates until she was in the shadows under the catwalks leading up to the ventilation system.

River turned and grabbed the piping and began climbing. She hoped there was no video surveillance of the area. If so, she should have had company already.

Rolling over the catwalk, she took the stairs up to the highest level before grabbing hold of the piping and climbing it up to the vent. It was small, but she wouldn't have any problems sliding through it. They didn't even have a grill over it. Holding on to the pipe with both hands, she stretched her legs out until she could slide them in, then pushed off letting the rest of her body follow. She moved back about ten feet into the vent before she leaned back and took a deep breath to calm her shaking body. She had never been so scared in all her life. The only thing keeping her going was the knowledge Jo and Star had to be even more scared than she was.

River crawled until she reached an intersection in the vent. Here it was high enough, she could actually stand up straight. She guessed whoever built it was a lot smaller than the creatures on it now.

They would have a hard time crawling as each one of them had to be over eight and a half feet tall and almost as wide. Moving to the left which she hoped was the direction the creatures had headed when they took Jo and Star, she followed the ventilation system for hours marking sections as she came to them with a permanent marker. Luckily she had always been good with directions, probably because she had traveled so much her whole life. It almost reminded her of the passageways under Paris, she, Star, and Jo had explored one summer.

River almost cried out with relief when she saw a schematic of the ship attached to one intersection. Pulling out one of her knives, she pried it off the wall. Sinking down, she looked over the map. It looked like there were some type of holding cells two levels up.

If she followed the ventilation system another hundred feet to the left there should be a vent leading up to the next level. She needed to do this again at the next level to get to the one she wanted. Sliding the stiff map into her shirt, she moved off to the left.

Sure enough, she came to a vent that went straight up. It was narrow, but it had what looked like foot holds. Grabbing hold of the first rung, River began climbing.

River spent the better part of the next three hours moving through the ventilation system. She had made it to the level with the holding cells. It had taken her longer to climb up to them than she expected. They were much further apart than she expected. Once she had made it to the level she wanted, she had paused to rest and get something to drink.

At first she was leery of what was in the bottle, but on smelling it and then finally taking a sip she was relieved to find it was water. She drank half the bottle before realizing she needed to conserve what she had. Closing her eyes, River felt the fatigue take over her body.

She needed to rest before she moved any further. She had been up for over seventy-two hours between arriving back in the States and her long flight and drive. Then there had been the wait in the shuttle until everyone had left.

Leaning her head back against the cold metal River felt a shiver run through her body. She had no idea how they were ever going to get home. No one would even begin looking for them for at least three months when they didn't return from the mountain. By then, who knew where they would be.

Shaking off the depressing thoughts, River focused on finding her friends first. She had to make sure they were safe. Her last thought as her body shut down was that she would worry about the rest later.

River woke disoriented. She hadn't meant to fall asleep. Taking a drink, she rubbed her eyes, trying to get them to focus. She wasn't far from the first row of cells. She figured she would leave her duffel bag here and check out each cell through the vent until she hopefully found Jo and Star. Shrugging the bag off her back, she checked to make sure all her knives were securely fastened so she didn't make any noise.

Standing up, she moved to the first cell. Peering through she saw it was empty. Moving to the next one she found the same. On her third cell she saw a familiar pink-and-white comforter lying across what looked like some type of bed. Peeking around the room River waited a good five minutes, listening.

"Jo, I'm scared," Star whispered. "Do you think they are going to hurt us?"

"I don't know, baby," Jo replied softly. "I hope not."

"Psst. Jo, Star," River called out softly.

"River?" Star whispered excitedly.

River pulled the vent grill up. Man, whoever designed these cells must have been thinking whatever was going to be in them would be too big to fit through the opening. It was a perfect fit for River's, Jo's, and Star's petite figures.

"You alone?" River asked quietly.

"Yes. They only come by once a day. They bring us something to eat and drink, then don't come back again until the same time the next day," Jo replied.

River was surprised. She didn't realize they had already been in here that long. She had fallen asleep earlier in the ventilation system but hadn't thought so much time had passed. She felt guilty at having slept so long.

"When will they be back?" River asked huskily.

"Not for another eight hours by my calculations," Jo said.

River laughed softly. Jo was always the level-headed one of the three of them. River slowly lowered herself through the vent opening and dropped lightly to her feet. Star rushed off the bed and wrapped her arms around River tightly.

"Oh River, you shouldn't be here," Star cried softly.

"Oh? And where else do you think I should be?" River teased softly pushing Star's hair back. "Whatever adventure we go on, we go together," River said softly repeating a mantra they had said since they had become friends.

Jo smiled through her tears. "Yeah, but even we aren't stupid enough to have invited you on this one."

"Well, I wouldn't want to be anywhere else without you," River said. "Now, we need to think about how we are going to get out of here and back home."

"What do you suggest? If we are on a spaceship, and I have to believe we are, God only knows where we are. Even if we were able to get off, where would we go? It's not like any of us know how to fly one of these things," Jo said sadly, sinking down onto the bed.

"Can you understand anything the creatures are saying?" River asked, trying to think of ways to get the girls in a fighting-back mood. Usually it was Jo who was the one shaking everyone up out of the doldrums. This was a new experience for River.

"Yes. They gave us some type of translator to wear," Star said, pulling her hair back to reveal a device that looked almost like a small hearing aid.

"I need one. I've been scouting the ship. If worse comes to worst, we can disappear into the ventilation system until we can figure out a way to get off this boat," River said holding out her hand.

Star handed her translator to River. "What should I tell them when they discover it missing?"

"Tell them it fell in the toilet," River grinned. "I bet they've dropped stuff down it before."

Jo laughed. "You are so bad." Sighing, she couldn't help but admit, "I'm glad you're here, River."

River smiled softly. "Me, too. If I am going to be hanging out here some I need to use your bathroom. I left my duffel bag up in the vents a few cells down. I figured I could spend part of the day with you and the other part doing reconnaissance. I need you two to stay here just in case someone decides to put in a surprise visit. I'll leave you some of my knives just in case you need them. Whatever happens, don't be afraid to use them," River added seriously.

Jo and Star nodded as they took the knives River handed them from her boots. They knew this was for real, and they wouldn't get a second chance if they hesitated. River used the bathroom to freshen up and refilled her water bottle.

The three of them talked for the next few hours planning different strategies. River had Jo copy the map she had of the ship, and they made plans on where to meet if they had to disappear into the ventilation system. They had three places they set where they would meet if they should get separated from each other.

Jo insisted River get a couple hours sleep, and she would wake her an hour before their next scheduled visit from their captors, so she could hide. River was going to stay close to make sure the translator worked before she would explore more.

Over the next two weeks, they did the same routine. River began having Jo and Star explore the vents to get familiar with the ship while she stayed with one or the other. They figured she could cover up with the bedspread and act like she was sleeping if the creatures came back early.

So far, they had been left alone. It wasn't until the beginning of their third week of captivity that they knew something major was happening. The ship jerked and shuddered, tossing them to the floor as the lights in the cell dimmed.

"What's happening?" Star asked, frightened. She gripped the edge of the bed trying to keep from falling again.

"I don't know. I'm going to go check it out," River said. "Give me a boost."

Jo and Star stood and cupped their hands, giving River a boost through the vent. River closed the vent grill before whispering, "I'll be back shortly."

The sisters nodded as they staggered under another shudder. The ship moaned, then everything seemed to become deathly quiet. Moving over, they sat on the edge of the bed, holding on to each other as they waited for River to return.

Chapter 3

River moved swiftly through the vents. She was a pro at navigating her way through them now. She had even pack-ratted items she thought might come in handy. She had food and water stored throughout the ship. She had found a storeroom filled with weapons.

She had taken as much as she thought she could get away with and hidden them in strategic places as well. Her biggest find had been what looked like explosives. She figured they could always find a good use for those. Moving down, she followed a group of creatures running toward the shuttle bay. They seemed to be very excited about something.

Running she made the quick climb down the vents until she came to the vent she had originally slipped into almost three weeks before. Staying to the shadows she moved quietly out onto the catwalk using the pipes to move around. There was a large square duct hanging down she could hide behind, but be close enough to hear what was going on as she would be almost directly above them. Crossing the thick metal beam she made her way across and hid behind it just as the huge creature that obviously was in charge stormed into the shuttle bay with almost twenty armed men following him.

Another ten men stood surrounding a shuttle with their weapons drawn. A small explosion caused the platform at the back of the shuttle to open. The men rushed in.

A few minutes later they came out, followed by a group of almost a dozen men. River caught her breath at her first look of the men. They were much different than the creatures that had captured Jo and Star. They were tall, about six and a half feet, but had long, black hair pulled back at their necks.

They were all dressed in leather pants and had on different colored shirts except for the one in the front who was older and wore some type of formal cloak. They were so handsome River would have to call them almost beautiful.

They appeared almost human in form. She couldn't tell what it was about them from this distance, but she knew there was something different about them. Maybe it was their builds which were very muscular or the way they carried themselves, but something was different.

River watched as the huge creature named Trolis walked up to the man in the long cloak and hissed at him.

"So, *Krail* Taurus, we meet again. This time there will be no peace negotiations," the huge creature hissed.

"Trolis, you have broken the treaty signed by your people by attacking an Alliance vessel on a diplomatic mission," *Krail* Taurus replied calmly. "This will be seen as an act of war."

Trolis grinned nastily before replying, "No, *this* will be seen as an act of war."

Before anyone knew what Trolis planned, he swung a double-edge sword and sliced the older man across his neck severing his head clean off his shoulders. The other men roared with rage and moved to attack. Suddenly, the ten men surrounding them opened fire and all the men dropped to the floor.

River shoved her fist into her mouth to keep from crying out. Silent tears coursed down her cheeks as she watched all the men drop. She almost fell from her hiding place when she heard Trolis tell the men to drag the men to the holding cells.

They aren't dead, just unconscious! She thought with relief.

She waited to hear what else Trolis had to say. She needed to know what he planned on doing to the other men. If he planned on killing them, she was going to have to tell Jo and Star they were moving up their attack on the creatures.

"Commander Trolis, what do you want us to do with the others?" one of the creatures hissed out.

Trolis swung his large head back and forth. "Two of the men are part of the royal family. I think a demonstration of who is in charge is necessary. Strap them to walls. Take the younger one with the red shirt and secure him to the center of cell block eight. I want the others to watch as he is gutted. I have plans for his older brother to suffer."

"Yes, commander," hissed the creature.

Trolis called out to two other creatures, "Clean up this mess."

River watched as Trolis walked out of the shuttle bay. She moved back along the metal beam, climbed back into the vent, and took off at a run. She had to let Jo and Star know about what happened and get to cell block eight before they had a chance to kill anyone else. She didn't know why, but she knew those men were their only hope of finding their way off this ship and back home. They had to free them.

* * *

"Torak," a voice called out hoarsely.

Torak shook his head to try to clear it. He focused on pushing the pain in his chest where he had taken a blast from the stunner. Looking up, he saw all his men chained to the walls, most of them just regaining consciousness. He looked up to see he was chained as well by both his arms and legs. Looking around, he frowned when he didn't see his younger brother, Jazin, with the others. His eyes narrowed when he saw Jazin chained to bars in the center of the room.

"Is everyone else here?" Torak asked harshly.

He was furious. The Alliance had a treaty with the Tearnats. He knew Trolis was a deadly opponent. He had fought against him in the wars before the treaty had been signed. He had not known Trolis had gone rogue until recently. The wars had ended two years before, and a tentative peace had been achieved with the Tearnats. Trolis had been a commander during the war and was the second son of the ruling family. He had not been happy with the decision to end the war, even though the Alliance had vastly outnumbered the turnouts in both technology and in warships.

Made up of over twenty different galaxies, the Alliance provided safe passage and support to ships traveling between the galaxies. Torak was a member of the ruling family of the Kassis star system. They were one of the most powerful members of the Alliance.

His people were very advanced technologically and had the most powerful warships. He, his younger brother by three years, and ten of his best men had been on a diplomatic mission with the head chancellor of the Alliance, *Krail* Taurus of the Dramentic star system. They had been on the chancellor's shuttle on their way to intercept Torak's warship, the *Galaxy Quest*, when Trolis had fired upon them, taking out their engines.

The chancellor had insisted they allow the shuttle to be taken and felt confident a diplomatic solution could be reached. Now the chancellor was dead, and he and his men were prisoners. His only hope was that the emergency signal he had sent out to his brother, Manota, would be received. If so, Manota might be able to reach them in time.

Torak's eyes narrowed when three of Trolis' men came into the room. He recognized one of them as Progit. He had fought against Progit and given him a nasty reminder of their encounter by cutting off one of his arms. Progit hissed loudly when he saw Torak. If the Tearnats could grin, Torak could have sworn Progit had one on his ugly face.

"So, we meet again, Kassis scum," Progit hissed. He pulled up his double-edged sword and made as if he was inspecting it.

"Progit," Torak replied. "You are much more confident when you have me chained. Release me, and we can settle what we started three years ago," Torak taunted the huge creature.

Progit just hissed. Pulling his sword, he swung it around before letting it cut a thin line across Jazin's cheek. Blood began pouring from the wound.

Torak growled. "Your battle is with me." He strained against the chains holding him.

"Not this time. This time Trolis has given me the right to extract revenge. I am going to start by gutting your brother in front of you. I'll cut him up into little pieces, one piece at a time, so you can hear him scream. Then, I am going to do it to each of your men. By the time I am finished, you will know exactly what you can expect," Progit hissed with satisfaction.

Torak growled louder. "I'll kill you."

Progit just grinned as he nodded to the other two creatures with him. "Pull him tight. I want him to feel every cut I make in him. I think I will take his arm first."

Jazin looked at Torak with a grim expression. Holding his head high, he spoke calmly. "I will meet you in the next life, brother. Fight well."

Torak looked at his younger brother, feeling overwhelming despair at the thought of watching him die such a painful death. "Die well, brother. Until we meet in the next life," he whispered.

Progit hissed his amusement. "So touching. Let's see how well he screams as he dies." Raising his sword above his head, he let out what could only resemble a malicious laugh.

* * *

River was out of breath as she raced through the vents. She grabbed her duffel bag as she swept by the entrance to the cell holding Jo and Star. They would need to hurry.

Pulling the vent grill out of the way, she reached down and said one word. "Now."

Jo and Star stared at her for just a moment before they nodded. Jo cupped her hand and lifted Star up through the vent. River reached over and helped her through the opening before they both reached down and grabbed Jo's hands as she jumped pulling her up as well.

River pulled two weapons out of her black duffel bag. She handed Star a miniature crossbow she used during her performances. She also gave her the twenty arrows she had to go with it.

"Make each shot count. Remember to aim for the throat or between the eyes. They have a thick bone covering their chest. I don't want to take a chance of the arrows not going through it. Jo, take the staff. Push the center button, it extends and has blades on each end. You are the best with that. They have some men captured in cell block eight. They are going to kill them, so we have to move now. Remember our plan. We'll take out any creatures in cell block eight, then head to our spots to shut down the lifts. I'll take out the engine room. Star, you head down to block all the entrances out of their living quarters. That should take care of almost half the crew. Jo, you make sure all lifts coming up to the shuttle bay are blocked. We meet in forty-five minutes at the vent leading into the shuttle bay. Remember to kill as fast as you can. Don't think," River said, looking at each of her friends. Now they were taking action she was calm. She would probably bawl like a baby if she lived through this.

"Do you think the men will help us, River?" Star asked hesitantly as she pulled the arrows across her back.

"Yes. I don't know why, but I feel like they are our only hope. The huge creature cut one man's head clean off, Star. He plans on killing all the rest of them. I don't know why, but I feel like we have to save them." River looked into Star's eyes before turning to Jo.

"Well, let's go kick some alien ass," Jo said with a smile. "Hell, if I'm going to die today I plan on taking as many of those assholes with me as I can."

"Showtime," the three girls said as they linked their hands. It was their favorite saying right before they were to perform.

Heading down the vent, they quietly came up onto cell block eight. Jo lifted the grill. It was located in a small unlit corner of the cell. This cell was much larger than the others.

River jumped down, crouching low until she was sure she hadn't been heard. Nodding up to Jo, she stepped aside as Jo lowered herself down, followed by Star. Nodding for each sister to take a side, they had decided River would come up the middle. It gave her more freedom to throw her knives with both hands.

With River holding up a hand, the girls listened as the one-armed creature talked about how he was going to kill each of the men before killing the man fighting against the restraints. River heard Star catch her breath when the young man said good-bye to his brother. That was all the three of them needed to hear to know they were making the right decision.

Torak watched as Progit raised his sword with a harsh laugh. He refused to look away from his brother's face. Just as Progit was preparing to bring his sword down to sever one of Jazin's arms, he froze in place. Torak watched in disbelief as he turned halfway around, then backward onto the metal floor, a knife protruding from between his eyes. He jerked when the other two creatures, who had been on each side of his brother, met the same fate.

Glancing up with undisguised hope, he softly called out. "Manota?"

River wasn't sure what to do when the man tied to the wall called out for someone. She looked around the room to see who he was talking to but didn't see anyone else. Nodding to Jo and Star, she moved slowly into the room. They would cover her back if these guys turned out to be bad too. Pulling her short swords from her back, she held one in each hand as she moved into the light.

Torak's breath caught in his throat as he watched a figure move cautiously out of the darkened corner. He had expected his middle brother, Manota. He had not expected to see the most beautiful female he had ever seen walk slowly out of the shadows carrying two battle swords. He watched as the female stopped just inside the room. She looked at the three Tearnats first, moving over to them and kneeling down to make sure they were dead. When she was satisfied they were she pulled the knives out of their foreheads with a disgusted look on her face, wiping the blades gingerly on their clothing. She then slid the knives into her boots.

Rising up, she glanced at him briefly before moving her eyes over each of the men watching her so intently. She moved to stand in front of Jazin looking up into his eyes. She slid one of her swords into the harness on her back before slowly raising her hand to the cheek with the blood on it. Torak growled low when she reached up. The female froze, then turned to stare at him a moment before she turned back to his younger brother.

River's heart had almost broken when she heard the man standing in front of her say good-bye to his brother. When she had looked at him after making sure the green scaly creatures were dead, she had been horrified at the blood running down his cheek. She had put one of her swords up so she could pull out a tissue to see how bad the cut was.

It had shaken her when the man on the wall growled at her. She had looked back at him to make sure he was still chained. She had to make sure she, Jo, and Star would be safe before she released any of them. What she hadn't expected was the immediate response she felt to him. It was as if her body knew him. She had to fight not to run to him and release him. Shaking her head at the craziness of it, she turned back to the younger man chained in front of her. Gently wiping the blood away, she was relieved to see it was just a thin, shallow cut. She had had plenty of cuts to know what a bad one looked like.

The man chained to the wall was watching her intently, following every move she made. She figured he was the leader of the group since the one-armed creature had been addressing him and not the others. It also seemed the other men looked to him as well, and she remembered him being next to the man in the shuttle bay who was killed.

She needed to know if she could trust him enough to help them. If not, she didn't know what they would do. She sent up a silent prayer she was making the right choice. Calling out softly, she motioned Star and Jo to come into the room.

"Star, see if you can stop the bleeding and make sure it isn't too bad. Jo, see if you can figure out how to open the locking devices on the chains, but don't unlock them until I ask you to," River said as she turned toward the man who had growled at her.

* * *

Torak heard a murmur ripple through his men as two other females walked out of the shadows. The smaller female was carrying a small crossbow. She held it tight in front of her, moving it back and forth as she surveyed the room. The third female was slightly taller than the other two females, but not by much. She was carrying a double-bladed staff which she held out in front of her. Torak was shocked. The first was nodding to the other two who took up positions in different parts of the room. He again felt the overwhelming need to rip the chains holding him loose and drag her to him. She was his. When she had reached to touch his brother, he had growled out of primal reaction to his female touching another male, not fear of what she might do to his brother. It shook him to feel so possessive and protective of a creature he had never seen before until now.

He watched through narrowed eyes as the female came closer to him. "Do you understand me?" she asked softly, studying his face intently.

He nodded, not trusting his voice to work right with her so close. He wanted to growl at her for putting herself in danger. He wanted to drag her to him and hold her close. But most of all he wanted to take her right then, right there, so no other male could claim her. Instead, he contented himself with a brief nod and an intense stare.

"My name is River. The one standing in front of your brother is Star, and the one over by the console is Jo. We need your help to get away from these creatures. Can you help us?" River asked.

She couldn't resist reaching up and gently pushing a strand of thick, black shoulder-length hair away from his face as she waited for his answer. He towered over her by a good foot or more. There was something about him that drew her to him. She shook her head in confusion at the idea of being attracted to this man. It was so unlike her. She had never felt this type of awareness to any male before back home.

Frowning, she looked up into his dark, almost midnight black eyes again, waiting for his answer. They were eyes that she could drown in, if she wasn't careful. Her fingers stilled as she absorbed the sculptured frame of his face. His eyes were outlined by thick black lashes that matched his hair. He had a broad forehead. His strong, square jaw was covered with a dusting of dark hair. His nose was slightly broader than the average humans but not by much, and his lips were full, especially the bottom one. His skin felt warm to her touch and was the color of her coffee when she used a little creamer in it.

He looks good enough to drink, she thought distractedly.

Torak's breath caught in his throat as the female reached over and touched his face gently with the tips of her fingers. He turned slightly so he could breathe in her scent. His eyes shimmered with a strange light as she jerked her hand back, flushing at doing something so intimate with someone she didn't know. He could not control the soft growl that escaped his throat at her withdrawal.

"I am Torak. Release us and we will help you," Torak answered softly, almost mesmerized. He looked deep into River's eyes, drowning in their intense deep blue. He silently demanded she obey him.

River shook her head. "I need your word you will help us get home and won't hurt me or my sisters. We *will* kill you if you try to hurt us. If you give me your word, we'll release you."

Torak looked at River with an amused look on his face. She fascinated him. She asked for his help while threatening to kill him and his men if they tried to harm her or her sisters. He glanced at the other two females who stood waiting for his answer.

Frowning, he wondered who these females were and why they were there. How had they come to know how to use weapons the way they did? He had never seen their species before, so he knew it was from a galaxy they were unfamiliar with, but where?

He looked at his younger brother who had not taken his eyes off the female in front of him. It appeared Jazin felt the same effect for her as Torak had for the female standing in front of him.

Looking back at River through narrowed eyes, Torak nodded. "We will give you safe passage home. Release us."

River backed several paces away from him before turning and nodding to Star as she moved past her. "Jo, on my mark."

Torak growled softly when he saw River move silently down the darkened corridor out of his sight. He strained against his restraints, trying to control the fury building in him. How dare she disobey him! Jazin's growl was louder, and his eyes flashed as Star moved away from him. He fought against his restraints, trying to watch where she went.

"Now," came a soft call just before the female named Jo hit the release button on their restraints.

Before they knew what was happening, she was running on silent feet down the darkened corridor where River and Star had disappeared. Jazin growled as he spun and raced down the corridor after the females. He slid to a stop as he watched Jo's feet disappearing through the vent opening. Torak was right on his heels, growling up at River.

River leaned over the opening, staying far enough back the men below couldn't grab her. "We'll meet you in the shuttle bay in forty-five minutes if all goes well. If one or more of us aren't there by the time you are ready to leave, go anyway. There is no sense in taking the risk of all of us getting caught."

"You will come down here now. You will stay with us where we can protect you," Torak snarled up at River.

Torak wanted to wring the female's neck. She had no idea how much danger she was in. She was a female, not a warrior. It was he and his men's responsibility to protect them, not the other way around. He couldn't wait to get his hands on her once they were safe. He would teach her who was in charge.

River raised her eyebrow. "In case you forgot, we just rescued your butts. We have some things to do to slow the ugly green dudes down a little. You *can* fly one of those spaceships, can't you?"

"Of course we can. You need to stay with us so we can protect you," Jazin insisted, looking up at Star who had bent over to peek down on them. Star blushed a bright red as she saw him looking up at her so intently and pulled back into the vent, earning a deep growl from Jazin.

"There are some weapons in cell block three under the bed. Now hurry. I don't know how long we've got before they find out we killed their friends. Remember, forty-five minutes." River slid the grill back over the cover and took off running for the engine room, ignoring the snarling demand for her to come back.

* * *

Torak was furious. Never had a female disobeyed one of his commands. Hell, none of his men disobeyed a direct command. He looked at his men fiercely before taking a deep breath.

"Let's go. We get the weapons, then head for the shuttle bay. Jazin, see if you can get a communications link open to Manota. I want him here now!" Torak bit out in frustration.

Jazin could barely contain his own fury. The female named Star was too small, too delicate, too female to be doing something as dangerous as killing Tearnats. He moved to the console and quickly hacked through the computer system to their main communication console, sending out a beacon for their warship. Setting it to send out a continuous signal, he followed the others to get the weapons the females had told them about.

* * *

River set the charges for the explosives to go off in five minutes. She would have to hurry to get far enough away so she wouldn't be caught in the blast. She had set different charges up high, so the top railing would collapse on the equipment below. She said a silent thank you to Bombing Bill for all his lessons on fireworks and explosives.

Bombing Bill had set up and managed all the firework displays for the circus, including the special effects during performances. He had worked for years as a special effects artist in Hollywood before joining the circus. He had always been patient showing River, Jo, and Star how to create fuses and stuff that frightened the daylights out of their parents. It hadn't stopped them from sneaking into his tent in between performances or on holidays to watch and sometimes help him build some of his displays.

Sliding back into the vent with the fuse, she lit it and took off at a run. She figured she had to get up two levels before the explosions began if she wanted to get clear of the automatic doors shutting off access. She had discovered during her trips through the vents there were several hatches that would close off the vents in case of fire. She had to get above the ones that would close when the engine room caught fire.

She was almost to the second level when she felt the ship shudder and a loud explosion sounded behind her. Breathing fast, she climbed the rings as fast as she could. She had to get out of the upward vent, or it would shut her in. She could already smell the smoke from the fire that had started.

She was almost to the top when the hatch slid shut blocking her way. Crying out in dismay, River stared in horror at the closed hatch. There would be no opening it. She would have to go back down and around. It would take her longer, and there was no way she would get to the shuttle bay in time.

She almost sobbed. They had made a pact. If one of them weren't there by the time they were ready to leave in the shuttle, they would go anyway. They could not take a chance of losing their only means of escape due to one of them. River quickly climbed back down the rings to the vent below. It was filling up with smoke fast. If she didn't get out of there she would most likely die from smoke inhalation.

Running as fast as she could, she pulled her shirt over her nose and mouth trying to keep as much of the smoke out of her lungs as she could. She felt tears wet her cheeks at the thought that this was how her parents had died. Moving toward the left, she went down another level before following the ventilation system to another upward tube.

She was growing tired from all the running and climbing combined with the smoke and stress. Grabbing the ring, she pulled herself up to the next level, rolling onto her back to catch her breath. She was now at least four levels below the shuttle bay. Depending on what other obstacles she encountered, she would be more than an hour behind the others.

Rolling to her hands and knees, she pushed herself up and began jogging. She had to make two more detours, including having to move out of the ventilation system at one point to get to the access she needed. She had surprised two Tearnats during her time out of the ducts and had barely had time to kill them before they sounded an alarm. By the time she made it to the shuttle bay vent she was almost three hours late.

Crawling as close to the opening as she could, she peeked down at the shuttle bay area. With a sinking heart, she saw it was full of activity. She noticed a large group of Tearnats in one section including the huge creature who had killed the one man. Lowering her head, she shook as silent tears flowed down her cheeks.

She had to know if Jo and Star had escaped. If they had been caught she would have to do what she could to rescue them. If they had been killed... She didn't even want to think about what she would do. River ran her wet cheeks against the sleeve of her shirt smearing dirt and soot from the fires across them.

Taking a deep breath, she pulled herself out of the vent and dropped down to the catwalk. She stayed in the shadows and moved silently down the piping along the wall until she was close enough to drop down on a set of crates. Lying flat for a moment to make sure she hadn't been seen, she rolled to drop down to the next one before sliding down between two others. She was small enough to get between them. None of the Tearnats would be able to fit. It was also dark enough no one would be able to see her. Crouching down, she walked slowly toward a group of Tearnats standing near the crates. Hopefully they would be talking about what happened.

"The prisoners have been secured for transport?" An especially large Tearnat asked.

River frowned. She didn't remember seeing him in all her travels through the vents in the last three weeks or more. Looking closely around at some of the others, her heart sank even further when she realized these were not the same ones she had seen before. It was only then she noticed additional men coming onto the ship from what looked like tubes opening off to the side of the shuttle bay. Biting down on her knuckles, she leaned against one of the crates.

Reinforcements, she thought in despair.

She pulled further back into the shadows trying to think. The Tearnat said something about prisoners and getting them ready for transport, which could only mean Jo and Star hadn't made it off the ship. They had been caught.

Shaking uncontrollably from fear, stress, and despair River struggled to get control of her emotions. Her going to pieces wouldn't help the situation. She took several deep breaths before pulling her swords out. She would do what she had to do looking with determination out the narrow opening.

* * *

Torak paced back and forth, coming to a stop when he saw one of his men approaching. "Have they found anything yet?" He waited impatiently for Kev Mul Kar, his Captain of the Guard, to answer.

"Nothing, my lord. The men have been searching the vents around the engine room, but the fire closed the hatches. If the female did not make it out there is a strong possibility she is dead. The vents are filled with thick smoke from the fire," the man replied softly.

He had been one of the men she had saved from the grisly death Progit had planned and sincerely hoped the female would be found alive. None of the men could believe what the females had accomplished in so short a time. The one named Jo had shorted out all the lifts above the cell block level, preventing any of the Tearnats in the upper levels from getting down to them. The one named Star had sealed all the emergency tubes large enough to handle the Tearnats' large bodies by blowing the hatches, forcing them to seal, while the one named River had taken out the engine room to prevent the Tearnats from following them should they escape in one of the shuttles.

Jo and Star had appeared on time in the shuttle bay, River had not. By the time Jo and Star had reached the shuttle bay, the *Galaxy Quest* had made an appearance. What had surprised Torak the most was that Manota was not the only one to board the ship.

Gril Tal Mod, Supreme Leader of the Tearnats and father to Trolis, had also boarded. He had been waiting to meet with the Chancellor to express his concern over his second son's decision to continue the war against the Alliance. When the distress signal had been received he and his men had insisted on joining Manota. Gril Tal Mod had been furious at the audacity of his son to so openly defy his orders to return to their home world.

Over the past two hours they had captured the members of the crew who were still alive, including a very angry Trolis. Torak and his men had dispatched quite a few of the Tearnats on their fight to the shuttle bay. What concerned Torak now was there was still no sign of River. Jo and Star had finally been convinced they would be more comfortable on board the *Galaxy Quest*, but only after he had promised them he would find River, no matter what, and let them know. Jazin had insisted he escort the sisters back to the warship.

"Keep searching. I want the female found," Torak said tensely. He refused to accept she had been killed.

River stood just inside the narrow passage between the crates waiting for the huge creatures to move off. She would try to work her way around the shuttle bay to see if she could find the prisoners they were holding. Just as she was about to make a move to another stand of crates she heard a familiar voice.

"Torak?" River called out softly.

Torak swirled around when he heard his name spoken softly. Running his eyes around the crates near him, he paused to listen carefully. "River?" he called out.

River shook with fear. Torak was standing out in the open with the other creatures, but he didn't seem to be worried about them. He had been walking around calmly with one of the other men from the cell block. Moving cautiously out of the shadows between the two crates, River kept her swords drawn in front of her in a defensive stance.

Torak drew in a breath when he saw her soot-streaked face and the obvious evidence of dried tears. He had never felt as overwhelmingly protective of another being as he did right then. Striding toward her, Torak paused in front of her, staring down into her dark blue eyes.

"You had us worried, little one," Torak said softly, not missing a single detail as he studied her. He could see the exhaustion in her eyes. "Sheathe your swords; we have control of the ship."

River looked at him a moment more before letting her eyes roam around the shuttle bay. She was still standing near the crates in case she had to make a break for it, still not trusting what her eyes were seeing.

Looking up at Torak with uncertainty, she asked softly. "Jo, Star?"

"They are safe. Jazin has taken them to my warship. I promised I would notify them as soon as you were found," Torak replied, waiting to see how River handled the information. He could tell she was ready to flee.

Looking at the huge Tearnat she had heard talking, she nodded toward where he was standing, watching her and Torak. "Who is that? Isn't he like the others?"

"That is Gril Tal Mod. He is the Supreme Leader of the Tearnats and a member of the Alliance council. He and his men were aboard my warship waiting to meet with the chancellor. He will take control of this ship and its prisoners," Torak answered. He could see the distrust flash through River's eyes before she nodded, slowly lowering her swords to her side.

"Lord Torak, would you introduce me to the female?" Gril Tal Mod asked behind Torak.

Gril Tal Mod had been startled when he had seen the female come out from between the crates. He had met the other two females, apologizing for their capture by one of his people when they had told him how they had come to be on the ship. He had enjoyed the brief talk he'd had with the two of them before Torak's brother, Jazin, had become overly protective and insisted on taking them to the other warship. This one, though, was totally captivating. He had listened as one of the men from Torak's group had explained how a blue-eyed female had killed three of the Tearnats' most feared warriors. Progit had been known for his cruelty. The fact this small, delicate creature had slain him defied all reason.

Torak turned as River tensed, blatantly staring at the huge Tearnat in front of her. "Gril Tal Mod, may I present Lady River," he said with a slight bow.

River stared at the huge creature before slowly taking a hesitant step forward. She bowed her head slightly before replying, "Sir."

All of the sudden a noise behind them caught River's attention. Trolis let out a roar before he broke free from the two Tearnat warriors who were leading him across the shuttle bay toward a shuttle. He flung the two Tearnats to the side, charging at Gril Tal Mod and Torak with the double-edged battle sword he had taken from one of the warriors. River didn't even think; she just reacted. Stepping in front of the two men, she threw one of her swords with deadly accuracy striking the huge Tearnat right between the eyes. He jerked back suddenly, the force of the sword, stopping his forward motion before he collapsed in a heap several feet from them.

River wasn't sure what would happen now. She held her other sword up in front of her, turning back and forth ready for anyone who would dare to attack. She swung it around as a group of both Tearnat and Kassisan warriors rushed toward her.

Shaking, she moved backward slowly, trying to get to the crates. She would go up the pipes to the ventilation system again, she thought wildly. She was breathing heavy as she watched the group of men stop and stare at her in amazement. She took another step backward, running into a hard body. Arms wrapped around her trembling form as she started to struggle.

"Hush, little one. You are safe," Torak said, wrapping one arm around River's waist while the other gripped the wrist holding the sword. "Release your sword," he whispered in her ear.

"I'm sorry. I'm sorry. I thought he was going to hurt us. I'm sorry," River kept saying over and over, the shaking in her body becoming uncontrollable as the stress of the past three weeks finally took control.

"You saved our lives, Lady River. My son would have killed not only me, but Lord Torak and any number of others as well," Gril Tal Mod said with sadness.

"Your son?" River choked in horror, looking at the huge creature in front of her.

"He was to be put to death for his act of killing the chancellor. You have given him a more peaceful death than he deserved. Have no regret for your action, child," Gril Tal Mod said, looking into River's deep blue eyes.

Gril Tal Mod nodded to Torak. "I believe we will not have any more problems from the other prisoners. Take your female and go in peace. One of our warships will be here shortly to help with repairs. I will return to the council chambers as soon as possible."

Torak nodded at Gril Tal Mod in gratitude. He knew the large creature would mourn the lost of his son privately. Increasing the pressure on River's wrist until she released her sword, Torak waited until it dropped with a clang to the metal floor before sweeping her shaking body up into his arms.

River looked at Torak with unfocused eyes. "I... I..." she began before her eyes closed, and she sank into blissful darkness.

Chapter 4

Torak held River's unconscious body tightly against his own as he made his way to the waiting shuttle. He called out to the rest of his men to follow. There was nothing left for them to do on the Tearnat's warship.

He moved to a seat, securing himself and River as the pilot slowly undocked. Looking down into her pale face, he couldn't help but wonder where she had come from and who her people were. She seemed so small and delicate, fragile even.

He ran his hand over her cheek, smearing some of the soot. It was amazing she had made it out alive. From what he had understood, the engine room was a mess. It would take several weeks to get it in any type of shape and months before it would be operational again.

The explosives she had set did their job in destroying the ship's ability to move. He had not had time to question the other two females. He had been too concerned with finding the one named River. He thought his heart was going to explode when she did not meet up with the other two as planned.

Now, as he stared down at her, he knew with certainty he would never let her go. Torak pulled River's body closer and kissed the top of her head, holding her face against his shoulder. No, he would never let her go. She had made him promise to take her home, and he would, to his home. It would now be hers. She belonged to him.

Manota met the shuttle as it docked with the warship. Once the shuttle docking bay had been pressurized the platform at the back of the shuttle lowered.

"Welcome, brother. The female is hurt?" Manota asked with concern, noticing how tightly Torak held the female to him and her pale complexion.

"I would feel better if the healer were to examine her. I believe she is just exhausted," Torak replied, moving swiftly toward the lift.

"Where did you find her?" Manota asked.

He knew Torak had been reluctant to leave the other warship until the female had been located. He did not know much except that Jazin had brought two other females over earlier, while he had been on the other ship fighting for control of it. Manota had yet to meet any of them. Looking down into the soot-covered face of the female his brother carried he wondered what had happened to her.

"She found me. She made it to the shuttle bay. I have not had a chance to talk with her about why it took so long for her to make it there. I suspect she had to find another way after the ventilation system she was traveling through was blocked," Torak said impatiently, waiting for the lift to stop at the medical level.

Striding down the corridor, Torak walked into medical yelling for the healer. He gently laid River down onto one of the medical unit's beds, smoothing back her hair.

"My lord, how may I help you?" Shavic asked.

Shavic was the resident healer on board the warship. A tall, slim man in his mid-thirties, he had a gentle, calm manner that worked well with the crew. His ability as a healer was often sought after by commanders of warships traveling for long periods in space.

"I need you to examine the female and make sure she is unhurt," Torak answered roughly.

He needed to know she would be all right. Until he knew he would not leave her side. He watched as Shavic pulled a large cylinder cover over River's body.

"Do you know what species she is?" Shavic asked curiously as he studied the female's soot-covered features.

Torak frowned; he hadn't thought about that. He would need to find out from the other two females what species they were. He had assumed since she looked close enough to theirs, she was compatible. He could not imagine being so attracted to a species that was not.

Shaking his head, he replied softly, "No, I do not know. I assumed she was close to our own from her general appearance. She is smaller, more delicate-looking than our women, but other than that she seems similar to our own."

In general, women in the Kassis system were taller than these females by almost a foot, averaging around the same size as the males. The women normally were given duties within the household and did not work outside of their houses which were made up of many different family units. Devoting themselves to the arts, family, and taking care of the needs of the men, the women accepted it was the males who were the warriors and protectors. The females rarely left their houses without the escort of a male. It was just safer that way. A female could request a house to accept her into it. If the house accepted her, the female was given a specific job to do. Never before had Torak seen a female warrior such as River and her sisters.

"I will do the best I can to see if she has any injuries," Shavic replied.

Shavic ran several scans over River, not finding anything that looked too unusual. She had no broken bones or other injuries. He was a little concerned about her lungs as she appeared to have suffered some smoke inhalation. He went ahead and did a repair to clear them.

"Other than exhaustion, I believe the female is well," Shavic said with a smile as he watched the look of relief flash over his commanding officer's face.

Torak listened with relief as Shavic gave his report on River. He turned when he heard her moan, softly walking over to stand near her.

* * *

River moaned again softly, turning her head from side to side. She was so tired, but she felt like she had to wake up. Something had happened. She moaned again as she tried to remember. She had been trapped in the ventilation system. She remembered having to find a different way to the shuttle bay. The shuttle bay—she remembered it and Torak. He had been there along with another of those huge creatures, then she had thrown her sword.

River's eyes popped open when she tried to roll over only to find her body was trapped in some kind of cylinder-shaped object. Struggling, she tried to pull her arms up enough to get her palms flat against the top to push it off her. Her breathing picked up as she began to panic.

"River, all is well. The healer is just making sure you are not injured," Torak said calmly, stroking River's hair, trying to soothe her.

River glanced wildly from Torak to Shavic and back again. Breathing heavily she whispered hoarsely. "Get me out of this thing."

Torak nodded to Shavic who raised the cylinder off River. The moment there was enough room to roll River did, dropping to the floor and pulling one of the knives from her boot. Still in a crouching position, she moved back along the bed holding the knife out low and slightly to the left of her, never taking her eyes off either man.

"River, you are safe," Torak said calmly, watching every move she made.

"So you say. Where are Jo and Star?" River demanded.

She was still disoriented and was upset she didn't know where she was. How long had she been out? Looking around the room she knew it wasn't like any of the rooms on the warship she had just spent three weeks learning every nook and cranny about.

"I will take you to them. Just put the knife away," Torak said, moving slowly toward River.

River hissed at him. "Stay back. I'll kill you if you come any closer. I swear I will."

Sweat beaded on her forehead at the thought of killing him. She was too close to the edge of reason. She needed to find a place she could rest without fear of being captured. She had to know if Jo and Star were safe like he said or if she needed to save them. Shaking, she could feel herself beginning to lose control over her emotions.

The sudden opening of the door distracted River. Torak took advantage of her distraction to kick out his foot, connecting with the knife in River's hand. Lunging forward, he grabbed River, yanking her down and under him where he could cover her body with his own and prevent her from reaching for another knife. A scream behind him was his only warning before small hands began pummeling his back.

"Let her go!" Star screamed as she attacked Torak, hitting him as hard as she could. "Let her go!" she cried.

Jazin pulled Star back into his arms, holding her tightly as she continued to scream and kick. Jo, who had been following closely behind them, ran to grab the knife Torak had kicked out of River's hand. As she swung around, a large pair of arms gripped her, pulling her against a hard body. Throwing her head back, she yelled furiously as she tried to break free.

"Jo, Star?" River called from beneath Torak's hard body. She tried looking around frantically, but all she could see was Torak.

"River!" Star cried out. She was crying so hard she had trouble breathing.

River suddenly went still under Torak. She looked up into his dark eyes for a moment before asking him softly to let her up. Torak hesitated a moment before releasing her. Pulling himself up, he kept his grip on River, pulling her to a standing position in front of him.

"You can let me go," River said quietly, not even looking at Torak.

She kept her eyes focused on Star who was now sobbing into Jazin's chest. Looking over at Jo, she watched as the man holding her reluctantly released her.

"Oh, River, we thought we had lost you," Jo struggled to say on a sob.

Jo started to pull away but was stopped by the hand still wrapped around her wrist. She let the knife she was holding drop to the floor. Only then did the hand release her but not before the man rubbed his thumb over her pulse. Startled, Jo looked up into the eyes of Manota. Blushing, she pulled away, moving toward River.

* * *

River gave a sigh of utter pleasure as she sipped the hot tea. She had showered, changed into some clean clothes, and eaten. She was still tired, but she felt better than she had in over three weeks. After the little incident in the medical unit, River, Jo, and Star had been escorted to a small room where River had taken the opportunity to wash the smell of smoke from her body. Jo and Star had filled her in on what had happened after they had separated to carry out their plan of attack on the Tearnat's warship. They told her how frantic they had been when River hadn't shown up as planned and how Torak had literally freaked out when River hadn't returned.

Torak had ordered an extensive search for River after Manota and Gril Tal Mod had arrived with reinforcements. After almost two and a half hours, Jazin had insisted Jo and Star return with him to the other ship to get cleaned up, eat, and get some rest. They had only gone after Torak had promised to do whatever he could to find River. Star kept blushing every time Jazin's name was mentioned.

"So, what's with you and Jazin?" River asked, not even bothering to hide the small, mischievous grin curving her lips.

"Nothing," Star said with another blush. "The arrogant jerk thinks he can boss me around."

Jo laughed. "He wanted her checked out from head to foot by the healer when we first came aboard the ship. When she refused, he started giving her hell for not listening to him in the ventilation system. You should have seen his face when she gave him the hand!"

"You didn't?" River said in mock shock. "You gave him *the* hand?"

Star sniffed delicately. "Yeah, a lot of good it did me. He didn't know what it meant."

"Yeah, you should have seen his face when Star explained it to him in explicit detail, then turned her back on him like he didn't exist any longer. I thought he was going to blow a gasket," Jo said.

Laughter pealed through the room as the girls let the stress of their capture and subsequent escape finally wash through them. For the first time in over three weeks they felt safe and were hopeful of finding a way back home. River lay back on the bed and listened as Jo and Star reminisced about what had happened as if it were now some great adventure and how they were going to see about incorporating some of the things they had done into their act when they got home. Sleep soon overcame her as she felt the warmth of their love surround her. They would watch over her so she could sleep, she thought.

* * *

Manota, Jazin, and Torak sat around the long table in the planning room.

"The females believe we will return them to their planet," Jazin growled out softly. His fingers clenched around the cup he held in his large hand.

"No!" Manota said defiantly.

Torak looked at Manota in surprise. "You too?" he asked.

Manota flushed. "The female named Jo. I do not understand the feelings I have, but I know she is mine. I will not let her go." Manota looked at his hands for a moment before he looked at Torak. "And you?"

Torak nodded in agreement. "The one named River is mine. I will not let her go. They will learn to adjust once we return to Kassis."

Manota and Jazin nodded, relieved. Manota asked quietly, "What do you know of the females?"

He had been astounded when he had entered the medical unit to discover the three females ready to do battle. When he had grabbed the one named Jo, he had felt an instant awareness on a primal level. It took all of his self-discipline to resist throwing her over his shoulder and hauling her away to his cabin.

"Not much," Torak said with a deep sigh. "After Trolis captured us and killed the chancellor we were taken to a holding cell where Progit was going to enjoy torturing each of us before he killed us. Imagine our surprise when he ended up with a blade between his eyes as did the other two Tearnats in the room. I thought you had received our distress signal and had come to our aid. I… we… were astounded when the female named River walked out of the shadows holding two battle swords in front of her like an avenging goddess. She insisted we help her in return for our release, even threatening to kill all of us if we tried to hurt her or her sisters," Torak said with a touch of amusement.

Manota looked at both of his brothers in astonishment. "She actually said she would kill you?"

Jazin replied with a laugh. "Yes, and after seeing what she did to Progit and the other two in a matter of seconds, I have no doubt she could have done it quickly."

"You have no idea," Torak murmured. "After I agreed to help her, she and her sisters disappeared into the ventilation system where they moved undetected, sabotaging the ship's lifts, emergency escape tubes, and engine room. River was trapped when the hatches closed unexpectedly on her and had to detour around to get back to the shuttle bay which is why she was so late meeting up with the other two females. I have never been as glad as when she called out to me. She was fearful of Gril Tal Mod and the other Tearnats on board, but she still reached out to me. When Trolis attacked—"

"Trolis attacked you?" Jazin and Manota both exclaimed in concern. They knew how strong and deadly he could be.

"Yes, he had been threatening to kill his father and myself. He knew he would receive the death penalty for killing the chancellor, and it would be a very painful death based upon the laws of his people," Torak said grimly.

"What happened?" Manota demanded.

It would have been a bloody fight if Trolis was involved. He hated the idea of Gril Tal Mod being struck down. He had liked the councilman.

"River killed him," Torak said, sitting back and watching his brothers' faces as they absorbed the news of one of Tearnat's most feared warriors meeting death at the hands of a small alien female.

"River? The female killed him?" Manota said, stunned, while Jazin just shook his head, grinning.

"Yes. As he came at Gril Tal Mod and me, she stepped between us, threw her battle sword, and struck him between the eyes." Torak grinned with pride as he thought about how his mate would be revered for her ability to kill two such powerful warriors as Trolis and Progit.

"Where do they come from?" Manota asked softly. "They must be a very powerful species to have females trained as such skilled warriors."

Chapter 5

River, Jo, and Star all laughed when one of the crewmen aboard the warship brought them dresses to wear. None of them ever wore dresses. Especially River!

It was hard enough to manage knives in jeans or her usual costume of a form fitting spandex outfit. It was almost impossible in a dress. She couldn't remember the last time she had worn one for that matter. She didn't even own a dress. Jo and Star had been just as bad. Flying through the air in a dress would get you killed, and pants were just more comfortable, especially when they would suddenly get the urge to bend in all weird ways to stretch their muscles. It was just a part of who they were.

They had sent the very puzzled crewman away with instructions on what they would wear. He had insisted on leaving the dresses even as he promised to return with the garments they requested. True to his word, he had returned an hour later with several pairs of black form fitting pants and matching tops from the clothing replicator. He had not looked very happy when he had left, but the three girls were ecstatic, quickly changing into their new clothes.

"Oh God, these are so soft! And look how they stretch," Star said as she did a back bend and looked up at the two between her legs.

"Now, this is the life. I can't wait to get home. How long do you think it will take to get there?" River asked as she did a few stretches, then went to a one-handed handstand.

"Will you two stop showing off! There isn't enough room in here for all three of us to become human pretzels!" Jo growled, stretching her leg up above her head.

After getting plenty of sleep over the past two days the girls were ready for some physical activity. They had never been ones to stand around idle.

"Let's see if they have a larger area. I'm sure they have some place where they must train or exercise during their long trips," Star said suddenly. She needed to fly. She loved being up in the air.

* * *

Soon the three girls had found someone to take them to the level of the ship reserved for training. He had been confused as he had escorted them down to the lower level before leaving them with the man in charge of training the warriors on board the *Galaxy Quest.*

Zoran looked over the three females standing in front of him in their gowns. They had reluctantly put the dresses on over their pants and shirt as the crewman who had dropped the clothing off said they would not be allowed out of the room unless they were dressed properly. The girls had just grinned at each other mischievously as they slid the gowns over their outfits knowing the dresses wouldn't be on for long.

"You wish to exercise?" Zoran asked hesitantly. He was not sure what type of exercise the females did that would require his training room.

"Yes," Star said, looking up at the high ceiling.

There were several beams located across it. Attached to the beams were different types of ropes and rings. With a little modification they could be used for trapeze performing.

"Do you have any other type of hanging bars that can be attached up there?" Jo asked, her gaze following Star's as she assessed the bars and platforms.

"Up there?" Zoran asked in disbelief. "You wish to go up there?" Zoran looked at the three females again.

"Yes," Star said patiently.

"Give me a few minutes, and I can have some of the warriors attach them." Zoran said in confusion.

"That's okay. We can take care of it if you just point us to some of your equipment. We will need you to set up the safety net if you have one. If not, we will just have to be extra careful," River said with a grin.

She had performed frequently with Jo and Star, and they could practice some of their old routines. She hadn't been this excited in months. It would be just like old times.

Zoran had shaken his head and pointed out the equipment they could use while he directed several warriors who were trained to help him connect the netting under the upper training level.

Jo, Star, and River headed for the equipment, picking out what they would use. Undoing their gowns, they let the material fall around them leaving them in their formfitting black skins. River had almost cried when she had seen her black duffel bag. Jo had collected it when she had headed back to the shuttle bay. River was missing quite a few of her knives, but nothing she couldn't live without. The only ones she mourned were her two short swords. Her mom and dad had given them to her on her sixteenth birthday. She knew one had been in the head of Trolis and she had dropped the other one when Torak had grabbed her. She had been unconscious when he had taken her from the Tearnat's ship.

Doing a series of bends and stretches, the girls warmed up before taking the equipment over to the ladder leading to the upper level. They were so intent on what they were doing, they didn't even notice the silence that had descended throughout the training room as they joked with each other.

Moving with ease from years of practice, they each walked out on the narrow beams as if they were strolling down a sidewalk. Lying down on the beams, they secured the swings and ropes where they wanted them.

Zoran looked in disbelief at the scantily dressed females, holding his breath as they moved over the narrow beams. He would be lucky if he didn't get killed for this, he thought in dismay. He had no idea what the females had planned as he had never had any ask for the things these females had asked for. He had not been paying attention to what the females were doing until he heard several of the warriors practicing swear under their breaths.

Turning, he had been stunned to discover they had discarded their long gowns for a form fitting outfit that showed every curve on their bodies. He couldn't have dragged his eyes away if his life depended on it. Each of the females had their hair pulled back in a braid and moved with a sensuous sway that spoke of pure pleasure.

Yes, he groaned under his breath, he would most decidedly be slain for this, if for no other reason than his thoughts. The other warriors were murmuring their delight in the females, watching in fascination as they connected the ropes and bars to the beam.

Turning, he growled low. "Watch them. I need to call for Torak," he said as he left.

It was only as he turned to go he realized he had probably, no definitely, said the wrong thing. *Watch them!* he thought, disgruntled, as if the warriors could peel their eyes away from three beautiful women dressed in clothing that only accented their curves. The warriors would be watching them all right, with lust. Moving into his office, he pressed the com button.

"Torak," came a deep voice.

"My lord, this is Zoran. I believe you should come down to the training level," Zoran said as his eyes followed the females.

"Is there a problem?" Torak asked, surprised.

"There might be, my lord. The three females are here," Zoran replied.

He couldn't have said any more if his life depended on it. His breath caught in his throat as he watched one of the females slid down one of the ropes and begin swinging while another did back flips on the narrow beams thirty feet above the floor of the exercise mats. He couldn't see the other female from the angle he was at. He was afraid to see what she was doing.

"On my way," Torak said tensely.

* * *

Torak called to Jazin and Manota to join him at the training level. He shifted when the lift he was in, paused and Manota and Jazin stepped in.

"What is going on?" Jazin asked curiously. He could tell something was wrong from the sound of Torak's voice.

"It seems the females are on the training level. Zoran just requested I come down. He sounded upset," Torak replied, his lips forming a firm, straight line.

The three brothers had not seen the females since they'd retired to the rooms given to them. The females had been either asleep, or Torak and his brothers had been in meetings with the councilmen from the Alliance over the past two days. It would seem they should have checked in on them sooner.

In truth, the brothers were trying to stay away from them until they received the council's approval of their request to claim the females. They would claim them with or without the council's approval; it would just make life easier if they had the council's support.

The three brothers strode down the corridor to the training level. The door opened automatically as they entered. Zoran, who looked more than a little flushed and distressed, met them at the door.

"Where are they?" Torak asked impatiently.

Zoran pointed up to the ceiling. "Up there," he said hoarsely, his eyes widening at what he was seeing.

River, Jo, and Star were having a ball. They were swinging through the air doing one of their most strenuous acts. Jo was hanging upside down, her ankles the only thing holding her to the swing. Hanging from her hands was Star while River was swinging from the other swing.

They moved faster and faster until River flew off the swing doing a triple flip in the air, barely missing Star who was doing her own flip. Star caught the swing River had just left while Jo caught River by her ankles swinging her up into the air only to have River double back up until she was standing on the swing above Jo. The girls continued for another twenty minutes before both Jo and Star did flying flips that had all the warriors holding their breaths and cringing at the same time as they fell into the netting. Bouncing up, the girls did a graceful flip off the netting to the floor below. River continued to swing on the bar high above.

Jo and Star grinned at Torak, Jazin, and Manota as they moved gracefully by them to pick up some small pieces of wood. Grinning again as they ran by them, they moved to different places around the training room. Torak, Jazin, and Manota were too busy watching as River did a series of flips and turns, letting go of the swing and catching it at the last minute. It was only when she called out that the men turned to see what Jo and Star were doing.

The two sisters had handed a number of wood pieces to several of the warriors around the room telling them to hold them up above their heads and not to move them. On the wood pieces, Torak noticed small circles marked in black. His eyes widened when, while studying one of the pieces of wood, a knife suddenly appeared inside the circle.

Torak's eyes jerked upward, and he watched as River flew from one swing to another, then to a rope, throwing knives as she went, sometimes upside down or in midair, at the targets his warriors held. Ten knives were imbedded in ten targets. The warriors slowly pulled the targets around, staring with pale faces at the knives, then up at the female flying through the air. Torak watched River's face as she moved through the air. She had a self-satisfied smile on her face, and she looked joyful as she glided, catching, twisting, and flipping through the air. Both of the other females watched River as she did one last flip, then grinned as Torak cried out in surprised when River appeared to fall.

Torak heard a peal of laughter from Jo and Star as River did a graceful flip, landing on her back in the netting to bounce up and do a front flip before landing on her feet. River walked, laughing, over to the edge of the netting, lying down and doing another flip only to land in Torak's arms.

Surprised, River sucked in a breath. "Hey."

Jo and Star skipped over to River, flushed from their workout, laughing with delight. "Oh River, you were great! You hit every target right in the circle!" Jo said excitedly.

Jo looked around when she heard Star give a startled squeak. Before she knew it, she was staring into Manota's angry eyes.

River glanced down into Torak's eyes, realizing he was holding back his own anger. "What's wrong?" she asked nervously. She didn't know why the brothers looked so angry.

"Do you three have a death wish?" Torak gritted out through clenched teeth, staring up into River's deep, blue eyes. He was still shaking from fear watching her flying through the air like that.

"Of course not. We knew what we were doing, didn't we?" River looked for guidance from Jo and Star. This is precisely why she avoided the opposite sex. She really didn't understand them at all.

Jo and Star started to say something only to be cut off by the men holding them. Torak looked at his brothers. They needed to divide the females. They got into too much trouble when they were together.

"Take them," Torak said harshly, tightening his grip on River when she began struggling.

"Take them?" River squeaked looking at Torak in growing anger. "Take them where? Where are you taking them? You can't. You promised to help us get home. What are you going to do? Jo? Star?" River called as she watched the other two men carry the struggling sisters out of the training room.

Zoran came over to where Torak was holding River. He looked decidedly paler than he had when the girls had first appeared in the training room. "My lord, what should we do with the knives the female threw?"

Torak looked at Zoran in disbelief. "Whatever you do, do *not* give them back to her," Torak said before he tossed River over his shoulder, hoping she didn't have any more knives hidden on her body.

River gave a startled yell, which quickly turned to a surprised humph, as she was flung over Torak's shoulder. Surprise more than anything held her in place as he moved through the line of warriors who stood looking at River's curvy ass.

Pushing herself up as he walked through the door, River yelled out behind her. "You take care of my knives! I want them back!"

Torak brought his hand down across River's ass, causing her to squeak in protest at the sharp sting. He'd had enough of this female thinking she was a warrior. He was ready to tie her up to his bed after he stripped her naked to make sure she didn't have any more knives on her.

He had never seen another warrior with as many weapons on his body as this female carried! The only way to make sure she didn't have any was to remove all her clothing so she wouldn't have any place to hide one. He shuddered as his body reacted to the thought of River tied naked in his bed. He would not wait for the council's decision. He would claim her before they reached Kassis, he decided.

River lay draped over Torak's shoulder, looking around as they moved down the passageway. She raised her hands palms out to the warriors they passed as if to say, *Beats the hell out of me what his problem is.* The warriors just stared as they passed. Torak was never so glad to get into the closed confines of the lift as he was as the doors closed. Lowering River to the floor, he turned her around before she could say anything and wrapped his arms around her, pinning hers to her side.

River looked up at Torak's tight features, deciding it might be wiser to just remain silent. She didn't know what he was so angry about. She also couldn't help, but wonder where he was taking her. She noticed he had said a different level than the level she, Jo, and Star's room was on.

River relaxed back into Torak's warm embrace resting the back of her head on his broad chest. She felt relaxed after her work out and pleased with how well it had gone. The three girls hadn't performed together in almost two years, so it felt good to know they could still do it. She had tried out some of her newer moves after Jo and Star had dropped down. She had told them what to do with the small pieces of wood-like material she had found.

Closing her eyes, she snuggled a little closer to Torak's body as the slight chill in the air cooled her heated body. River let her mind wander back to some of the different moves she would like to try. She had no idea as she snuggled closer that Torak was thinking of some moves of his own.

Torak bit back a groan as River wiggled closer to his body. The material covering her left little to the imagination when viewed from a distance, but held close like she was now it made his imagination ignite with all kinds of ideas. Closing his eyes, Torak pulled her even closer, sliding his arms up so the weight of her breasts rested along his arms.

Torak bit back an expletive as the doors to the lift opened on the level containing his own living quarters. Sweeping River up into his arms, he carried her down to his quarters, ordering the door to lock after him. Torak set River down and watched as she looked around with growing concern.

River didn't know what was going on, but she knew this was someone's, most likely Torak's, living quarters. She nervously pushed a stray strand of hair away from her face.

"Uh, Torak, why are we here?" River asked as she moved away from him with a nervous glance.

"What did you think you were doing down in the training room?" Torak asked, watching as River's eyes slid away from his bed.

River moved as far from the bed as she could which wasn't nearly as far as she wanted to. The room was not much bigger than her quarters. Moving to stand near a small table, she ran her trembling fingers over it.

River glanced at Torak before looking down again at the table. "Practicing. Jo, Star, and I were bored and needed some exercise. There wasn't enough room in our quarters, and one of the crewmen told us there was a training level. We thought we would check it out. It was perfect."

"You could have been killed!" Torak said, moving slowly toward River, who backed up until she was pressed against the wall.

"No, I wouldn't have. I've been doing those things my whole life. It was fun," River said defensively.

"Fun?" Torak exclaimed loudly. "Fun! I lost ten years off my life from your fun!"

River looked at Torak confused. "I don't understand. Why should you care about what I do? I mean, it wasn't like I was in any danger, and I wouldn't have hurt any of your men. I do riskier routines all the time. I…"

"Riskier?" Torak growled softly.

River stared up into Torak's eyes, unable to move. She couldn't speak with him standing so close to her, so she just nodded. Torak had placed both hands on each side of River's head, but now he placed them on her shoulders letting them slide down her. Without warning, he grabbed River by the wrists and turned her so she faced the wall. Putting her hands on the wall at shoulder height, he pulled her back around her waist until she had to use the wall to keep from falling forward.

"Stand like that," Torak whispered harshly in her ear.

"What?" River asked breathlessly. She didn't understand what he was doing until she felt his hands running down her body.

Torak ran his hands down River's body looking for additional weapons. He knew she would have more. From the little time he had spent with her, he realized she always had a multitude of them hidden somewhere on her delicious little body. He paused at the thin belt around her waist, pulling it free and letting it drop to the floor with a thump. He ran his hands over her ass, biting back a groan when she arched up into his hands.

River moaned as she felt Torak's hot hands moving over her. The material of the outfit she was wearing was extremely thin, and she could feel the heat of his hands as if they were caressing her skin. She let out a hiss and squirmed when he ran his hand between her legs.

"What are you doing?" River stuttered, flushing as the idea of his hands running over her body made her want to do things she had never thought of doing before.

Torak's jaw hurt from him clenching his teeth to keep the moans from escaping as he searched her. "Searching you for more knives."

"But why?" River asked puzzled. "I always carry them with me. Well, except when I go through the airports. I don't, then, because I don't want to get in trouble. I forgot once and it was a nightmare. Ricki had to come and explain everything. I thought Walter was going to have a heart attack. He locked me in his bedroom for almost two days until everything was cleared up. I made sure I never forgot to check again after that," River knew she was rambling, but it was all she could do since she was so nervous with his hands roaming her body.

"Walter? Bedroom?" Torak bit out, jealously.

"Yeah. If he hadn't been so good to me, I would have sliced him up a new one," River moaned as Torak ran his hand back up the inside of her thigh after he had removed the small knives attached to her ankles. "I think you have them all," she whispered hoarsely.

"I need to make sure," Torak replied huskily. His deep voice sending additional shivers through River.

River felt every point of contact as Torak stood up running his body up along hers. She choked when she felt something hard rub against her butt. When she tried to move away, she found herself turned and pinned against the wall with her hands above her head. River stared wide- eyed up into Torak's beautiful dark eyes, wondering vaguely if she should be struggling. She knew if she really wanted to get away from him she could, but right now she didn't feel like going anywhere.

Torak watched as River's dark blue eyes grew even darker. He had never seen such beautiful eyes before. They reminded him of the blue nebula with their swirls of blues, some so dark as to appear almost black. He gazed down into her almond-shaped eyes, watching them as he pressed his hard length against her. He saw her hesitate for a moment before her eyes grew heavy with desire. Torak felt a brief moment of triumph before he lowered his head to claim her lips with his in a savage kiss filled with desire and possession.

Chapter 6

River had never been kissed so thoroughly before in her life. She moaned and moved her body restlessly against Torak's, wanting more. She wanted to run her hands through his long, dark hair, to pull him even closer. Her breath caught as she felt him press his hard shaft into her stomach. Without thinking, River lifted one of her legs, wrapping it around his hip and drawing the hard shaft toward her feminine core.

Torak pushed himself against River, lifting her until the vee between her legs fit against his pulsing shaft. He shuddered when River lifted her other leg, wrapping both of her legs around his waist and arching her back against the wall, forcing him even closer. Grinding his hips up against her, he released her mouth and moved to kiss her jaw and neck.

"Oh, oh, oh..." River moaned over and over, twisting her hips in circles against him.

Torak changed his grip to hold both her wrists in one of his large hands so he could run the other one over her. He gripped her braid in one hand, forcing River to tilt her head to one side, giving him better access to her throat. River cried out and arched into Torak's mouth when he bit down on her neck. The sudden pain followed by his tongue running over it caused her womb to clench and her pussy to dampen in desire. Making love with Torak would be a wild ride, River thought vaguely, with a combination of pleasure and pain driving her crazy.

"Mine," Torak muttered, his voice husky with desire.

"I... Oh god, what are you doing to me?" River gasped as Torak's hand slid under her thin shirt to grasp her breast through the sports bra she wore.

"Mine," Torak growled possessively as he pushed the sports bra up, exposing River's distended nipple and rolling it between his fingers.

River let out a small scream as she felt her body tighten with need. "Oh god, you have to stop. Please, you have to stop," River said shaking her head back and forth.

Torak pulled his hand out of River's shirt. Gripping her chin in his hand, he stared into her eyes fiercely. "You are mine. Computer record: I, Torak Ja Kel Coradon of the House of Kassis, claim you, River, for my house and as my mate. I claim you as my woman. No other may claim you. I will kill any other who try. I give you my protection as is my right as leader of my house. I claim you as is my right by the House of Kassis. Computer end recording and file."

Torak looked at River as he said the traditional words that bound her to him. For all intents and purposes she now belonged to him as his mate. While he had other females in his household, he had never bound any of them to him. He had recorded his pledge and filed it. A copy would be sent automatically to the council and to the members of his house, showing he had bound River as his mate.

River stared at Torak in confusion. "What did you just do?"

"I have bound you to me. You are now my mate and belong to me," Torak said fiercely.

"I don't belong to you. I don't belong to anyone. I'm too young to belong to anyone and besides I don't want to belong to anyone," River whispered, suddenly feeling very, very nervous.

She could feel the awkwardness she usually felt around the opposite sex coming on. She was suddenly aware she had her legs wrapped around Torak's waist. River blushed and let go so she could slide them down to the floor. She was still trapped between Torak and the wall with her hands above her head.

Trying to look everywhere but at him, River muttered under her breath, "Please let me go."

She really was beginning to feel uncomfortable. She had never gone beyond first base with any guy before, and Torak's kiss alone felt like she had been halfway to third.

"You are mine, River. I have claimed you. You belong to me," Torak said arrogantly. He moved far enough back to look her up and down possessively.

River's eyes narrowed. Only once before had someone ever said that to her and looked at her that way. It had been some guy she had gone out with on a total of two dates, and he thought that entitled him to her body. River didn't like it then, and she didn't like it now.

Narrowing her eyes, she said calmly. "Take it back."

Torak looked surprised before replying. "No."

River glared at him coolly. "I said, Take. It. Back."

"And I said, no," Torak replied just as coolly.

"Fine. Your funeral," River said right before she lifted her knee and impacted it with Torak's exposed crotch.

Torak's eyes widened before he let go of River's arms which she brought down in a karate chop on his shoulders, dropping him to his knees. River had a moment of doubt when she kicked him in the chest, knocking the wind out of him. Twisting away from the pain and fury she saw in Torak's eyes, River realized she might have acted just a might hasty. Not knowing what else to do she headed for the door only to find it wouldn't open.

Torak groaned out. "You are going to pay for that," he gasped as he held his crotch with one hand and his chest with the other.

River looked around frantically, trying to figure a way out of the room before he recovered. Rushing to the bathroom, she ordered the door closed and locked it from the inside. Glancing around, she noticed a vent in the ceiling. It would be a tight fit, but she was sure she could wiggle into it. Standing on the toilet, she pulled the grill down and jumped, pulling herself through the small opening. Scooting back until she could reach the grill she pulled it back into place as she heard a loud thump against the outer door. Frightened, she backed up until she came to a junction leading to a larger vent. Moving on her hands and knees, she fled as fast as she could through the ventilation system. Oh God, she was back to living in the vents, she thought with despair.

* * *

"What do you mean, she's gone?" Manota asked in disbelief. "Where could she have gone?"

Torak ran his hand through his hair, flushing. He had finally had to break down the door to his bathroom only to find River gone. He knew the only place she could have gone was into the ventilation system. He had called to her over and over to come out, but she had not responded. When he had torn the grill off the opening so he could at least get his head up inside the vent to look around he didn't see her.

"She's in the ventilation system," Torak muttered, brushing his hand over his neck.

"And why is your mate in the ventilation system?" Jazin asked, puzzled.

"She wanted me to rescind my claim on her," Torak muttered softly.

"What?" Manota asked, irritated. "She wanted you to what?"

Torak turned and glared at both of his brothers. "I said, she wanted me to rescind my claim on her, and I refused."

Both brothers looked at Torak in shock. Never had a female refused a claim by a male, especially a claim by one of the ruling members. It was a great honor to be claimed by one of the ruling males. The female would receive much acclamation and be held with great respect and honor in any house she was in. Torak, as the next leader, was considered to be one of the greatest prizes, with many females asking to be in his house with the hope of being chosen. They didn't know what to think of a female actually refusing to being claimed.

"How did she get into the ventilation system?" Jazin asked curiously.

Torak just glared at his younger brother in frustration. Like he was going to tell them how the female disabled him and put one of the strongest warriors on Kassis on the floor like a sniveling first year.

"What of the other two females? What did you do after you took them from the training center?" Torak asked.

If at all possible they had to keep the three females apart. He hated to think of how much damage the three female warriors could do to his men and his ship. He had had a taste of their power on the Tearnat's warship.

It was Jazin's turn to flush and rub his hand across the back of his neck. "I took Star to another room and locked her in. She wouldn't quit crying as long as I was near her. I couldn't stand her tears any longer and told her I would return later once she had calmed down."

"What about you, Manota? What did you do with the female named Jo?" Torak asked in frustration.

"I took her back to her room," Manota said defensively. "What? She said she would never speak to me again and every time I tried to talk to her, she just held up her hand, not even looking at me. It was as if I didn't even exist!"

Running a hand down his face Torak groaned. These female warriors were going to be the death of them all. He had to figure out a way to find River and make her understand there was no changing his claim on her. He wouldn't change it even if he could. He had to admit a small part of him was impressed at her ability to disarm him. It didn't mean he would let it happen again, just that he was proud of having a strong female as his mate. Their offspring would be strong, he thought with a grin.

"What are you grinning about?" Manota asked disgruntled. "I thought you were mad at the female."

Torak grinned. "You have to admit life will be interesting with three such strong warrior women. Just think of how strong our offspring will be."

"Yeah, well, I just don't know if I will survive long enough to create them," Jazin muttered.

* * *

River's knees were killing her. She had crawled through what seemed like a ton of small vents off the main ones looking for Jo and Star. She had finally found Star on the level below the one she had been taken to.

"Star," River called softly. The room was dim with only a small light shining from the bathroom. "Star, are you awake?"

"River? What are you doing in the vent?" Star asked, puzzled, looking up from the bed at River who was gazing down at her through the grill.

"I, uh, I kind of beat Torak up, and he, uh, kind of got upset about it," River whispered back down at Star.

"You beat up the captain of the ship?" Star gasped before she started laughing. "Oh, River, what did he do to deserve that?"

"He said he claimed me or some such nonsense. You remember Billy Myers?" River whispered.

"Oh no, he didn't pull a Billy Myers, did he?" Star asked laughing.

"Yeah, he did," River laughed back, resting her chin on the edge of the vent. "I told him to take it back, and he said no, so I decked him."

Star laughed so hard she had tears running down her cheeks. "Oh, River, that's priceless."

Sobering up she looked up at River from where she lay on the bed. "River, I don't think they are going to take us home. Jazin won't let me see Jo either. He said they were going to keep us apart for a while until we learn to behave like females. I'm scared, River."

River looked down at Star. "Come on. It's time to find Jo and figure out how to get out of here. This is the last time we trust any guys."

Star looked up at River and nodded uncertainly. "How are we going to get out of this one?"

River reached down and grabbed Star's hand, pulling her up into the vent next to her. "Who knows?" River said with a grin. "As long as we're together again, who cares! Now come on, let's go find Jo. Maybe she'll have an idea and some food!"

Star grinned back. Maybe all they needed to do was show a bunch of macho males who was really the boss, she thought. It might be fun this time. Star pulled the vent grill closed and started crawling behind River.

* * *

The girls had been in the ventilation system for three days, moving from level to level and driving the men nuts. The vents were too small for the men to get into, and the girls were too smart to stay in any one place long enough to get caught. They now had a new challenge. Torak, Manota, and Jazin had stationed men in the larger emergency tubes in an effort to catch the girls.

Manota poured over the schematics of the ship while Jazin paced back and forth. Torak sat at the table in the conference room with his head between his hands, growling in frustration. They were supposed to be on Kassis tomorrow. He had no idea how he was going to explain his missing mate and her two friends to the council members who had requested they be presented to the assembly.

"Any luck?" Jazin growled, frustrated.

He had been livid when he had gone to check on Star only to find her missing. When he had sounded the alarm, Manota had gone to check on Jo and found her missing as well. They had been taunted by the females over the last three days with food, clothing, and blankets mysteriously disappearing from different rooms around the ship. Torak had been so concerned, he had posted additional guards to their weapons storage and even had men stationed in the emergency access tubes. They had found nothing— nothing but some haunting laughter that echoed throughout the ship and told them absolutely nothing. At this point, he was ready to pull his hair out.

Swearing loudly he stood up. "Where in the hell are they?"

River looked down at the men through the vent grill. All three looked exhausted. It was weird, but she almost felt sorry for them. River couldn't take her eyes off Torak.

He was so damn handsome it almost hurt to look at him. She was smart enough to know she wanted him in a way she had never wanted another man before. She just didn't like the way he had claimed her without asking her. She wanted to be romanced, not claimed like a car. She wanted to get to know him, not be told she was his. She wanted... him, just in a way she could handle.

She also had to come to terms with what it would mean to belong to him. She knew if she made the decision to accept him, she would never see Earth again, and she wasn't sure she was ready to take that jump. To never see her home, her friends, her world... She needed time to make that kind of decision.

"We arrive on Kassis tomorrow. How are you going to explain to the councilmen the disappearance of not only your mate, but the other two women?"

Jazin asked, leaning back against the glass window, the vast darkness of space behind him.

"I don't know. There is no way they can get off the ship. It is only a matter of time before they are caught," Torak said tiredly.

"Yes, but time is the one thing we do not have," Manota added glaring at the schematic in frustration.

There were miles and miles of ventilation system running through the ship. Even with the larger tubes cut off the females could bypass them using the smaller ones. It was a strategy they had never encountered before and would have to take into consideration. They were lucky it had been these females and not some other species bent on their destruction.

"I have no idea where they could be!" Manota said in frustration as he sat down at the table. "They could be anywhere. There are miles and miles of ventilation systems they could access that we can't. If they had been bent on our destruction we would be dead now."

"I have never seen a warrior clan as elusive as these females. I would not like to have to face their males if they are as good as these females," Manota continued.

River couldn't keep the grin from spreading across her face. They thought she, Jo, and Star were warriors? She couldn't wait to tell Jo and Star that. She wondered what the men would think if they knew she and the other girls were just circus performers. They had never had to battle anything worse than a strong cold or a bad boyfriend. Sliding back away from the vent opening, River moved silently away from the conference room and back to where Jo and Star were waiting for her.

"They think we are warriors?" Jo asked in disbelief.

Jo looked at River and Star and burst out laughing. They didn't even like to argue much less fight. They had only done what they'd had to do over the last month and a half because they didn't have a choice.

"So, what are we going to do?" Jo asked, looking back and forth between Star and River.

"I don't know. What do you two think?" River asked.

She already knew what she wanted to do. She wanted to get out of the vents. She was tired of living in them. She also wanted to be near Torak again. She didn't admit to the other girls, but she had spied on him over the last three days.

She flushed when she remembered watching him shower. She hadn't meant to spy on him while he was bathing, but she had been so mesmerized as he had removed his clothes she hadn't been able to look away. Later, she had watched him sleep.

On the second night, he had talked softly to himself. She had listened unabashedly as he pulled up a picture of her on the computer console in his room. He had re-enforced his claim on her. Only this time it didn't make her mad as she listened to him.

She heard something in his voice she didn't understand, but it sent a shiver of need down her spine. She had hidden her face in her hands, biting her lip to keep from calling out to him. Unable to leave him, she lay above him in the vent and watched him sleep for hours before she had quietly crawled away.

"I want to get out of these vents," Star said softly. "I miss Jazin."

Star looked defiantly back and forth daring either one of the other girls to deny their own feelings.

River let out a relieved sigh. "I guess that answers your question. We go back."

The girls decided they would make an appearance tomorrow morning in the shuttle bay. River would go out first with Jo and Star covering her back. They would meet with the council members and greet them as representatives from the planet Earth. River had recovered her black duffel bag during one of their excursions and planned on being decked out. Jo and Star would carry their signature weapons of choice.

They didn't know what to expect, but they hoped a little bravado went a long way because all three of them were scared shitless. None of them had talked about the difficult choice they knew they were going to have to make soon: stay or return home.

Right now, none of them felt like they could make that final, important decision without knowing more about the men who were causing them to have doubts about returning to their home world.

Chapter 7

Torak, Jazin, and Manota stood in the shuttle bay waiting for the councilmen to disembark from the shuttle. Torak shifted impatiently from one foot to the other. He had not expected the councilmen to board the *Galaxy Quest.* He had worked on all types of excuses as to why the females couldn't be presented to the council assembly right away. Now, all those excuses were worthless as the council had decided to bring the assembly aboard his warship.

Torak glanced at Jazin and Manota with a frustrated look on his face. Both the other men just shrugged their shoulders. They didn't have any idea of what to say and were just as frustrated as Torak.

"Lord Torak, may I present the council members," one of the council guards said, stepping back to let the councilmen approach.

Torak stepped forward and bowed to the councilmen before standing straight. "Gentlemen."

Grif Tai Tek stepped forward. Torak scowled as the tall councilman approached him. He bit back a curse. Tai Tek was a pain in the ass on a good day, and today was not a good day. He had been opposed to ending the war and had always been jealous of the Ja Kel Coradon name and the House of Kassis.

"Torak, where are the female warriors we have heard so much about?" Tai Tek asked looking around skeptically. "I do not see them."

Torak cleared his throat. "They are currently not available. It was our understanding we were to present them in the assembly room."

Tai Tek grinned wickedly. "Yes, well the council members were intrigued by the idea of women actually being warriors and did not want to wait. Surely they truly exist or was it just another way to try to make the House of Kassis appear something it is not?"

Torak's eyes narrowed, and he held his hand up to stop his brothers advance at the insult to their House. "They exist. We will present them at a later time."

Tai Tek looked directly at Torak before demanding softly. "I think not. Present them now or admit they are a make-believe stunt created by the House of Kassis."

Torak bit back a sharp retort. What he really wanted to do was challenge Tai Tek for attempting to smear the name of the House of Kassis but he couldn't do so without proof and without the females, he had no proof. Standing silently before the council, he glared at Tai Tek.

* * *

River, Jo, and Star had been watching what was going on from the beams above the shuttle bay area. They had secured ropes to the higher beams and had planned to make a dramatic entrance. Listening to the puffed-up pinhead below made River so mad she was ready to knock his socks off.

Who did he think he was ridiculing Torak in front of the other councilmen and his own men? Standing up on the narrow beam, River nodded to Star and Jo before letting out a battle cry Mel Gibson would have been proud of.

Startled, Torak swung around and looked up toward the beams above the shuttle bay. His breath caught in his throat as he saw River standing there looking down at him. She looked into Tai Tek's eyes before diving head first off the beam.

Torak let out a strangled cry as he saw her dive off the beam. Within seconds, Jazin and Manota both called out as they watched Jo and Star do the same thing. With utter grace and ease, River seemed to fly through the air before releasing the rope she had been holding to do a flip in the air and land on the floor of the shuttle bay.

Crouched down with one knee and with one hand down on the floor and her head bent, she didn't lift it until the other two females had landed right behind her. Only then did she slowly stand, drawing out her two short battle swords from the sheath on her back in slow motion. Looking up with her vivid blue eyes outlined in black, she stared with deadly intent into Tai Tek's eyes. Taking a step forward, the other two females stood up behind River. Star held a small crossbow in her hands while Jo held a double-bladed staff.

* * *

Tai Tek stood stunned. He thought he finally had Torak where he wanted him. None of the councilmen had believed the reports coming back from the *Galaxy Quest* about warrior females who had not only killed some of the fiercest Tearnats in the known galaxy but also single-handedly crippled one of their huge warships!

Tai Tek had been instrumental in getting the council members to come aboard. He did not want to give Torak a chance to find some females he could dress up and pass off as warriors or give some stupid excuse as to why he could not produce them. He wanted the council to see what a mockery Torak and the House of Kassis really were. When he had seen Torak and his brothers standing alone except for Torak's men he had felt a wave of bitter triumph flash through him. Finally, he would humiliate Torak and his brothers.

He had been waiting for Torak to admit he had made up the females when the war cry had resounded, echoing through the shuttle bay. Never in his life had he expected to see what he did when he had looked up. Almost fifty feet above the floor of the shuttle bay a small female stood upon a narrow beam glaring down at him, her willowy body clad in a form fitting black sheath. He watched in disbelief as she plunged headfirst off the beam, seeming to fly through the air before swinging up into a graceful arch and completing a flip to land facing the council. Just as quickly two other females had appeared as if by magic landing behind her.

A shiver went down his spine as she slowly stood to face the council pulling two short swords from behind her back. She moved with a grace that captured his attention. When he stared into her dark blue eyes, he felt like he could drown in their liquid depths. She was the most mesmerizing creature he had ever seen moving with confidence as she swung her swords in front of her, challenging anyone willing to stand before her. Tai Tek took a step back as she strode toward him with a deadly gleam in her eyes.

"Be very careful whom you insult, Tai Tek," the female said in a soft, lilting voice that held a thread of steel in it as she swung her sword, stopping a hairsbreadth from Tai Tek's neck. "My sisters and I stand behind the House of Kassis. To insult them is to insult us."

River stared at Tai Tek watching as he took a nervous swallow. She didn't remove her sword from his neck until he lowered his eyes. She had made her point. She would not tolerate him or anyone else insulting Torak, or his brothers.

Taking a step back, River turned toward Torak and bowed her head. "My lord," she said softly, glancing up at him with a mischievous curve to her lips and a twinkle in her overly dramatic made-up eyes.

Only after acknowledging Torak and his brothers did River turn to bow to the councilmen. By doing so, she was showing her allegiance to him and his brothers first. Standing straight she moved so she stood slightly behind him and to the left. She wanted to give herself enough room should she need to prove her ability to defend herself or protect those she cared about.

Torak looked into River's eyes as she glanced up at him. She had much to answer for when they were alone. He could think of a dozen different punishments he would like to give her, but all of them disappeared when she had looked at him just now.

Looking at the council members Torak said in a firm voice. "Council members, I present my mate, Lady River, and her warrior sisters, Lady Jo and Lady Star."

River let out a soft "humph" at his claiming of her so publicly. Torak smiled. The fact that she stood behind him now spoke volumes. She was his whether she was ready to admit it or not.

Torak watched as Tai Tek's face grew red with anger at his claim, but he wisely held his tongue. Torak knew he would have to watch Tai Tek closely in the future. Never before had he publicly challenged him, but Tai Tek was getting careless. His insult would not be forgotten just as his embarrassment at the hands of a female warrior would not be forgiven.

* * *

River waited until all the council members had boarded the shuttle before looking around the shuttle bay. She had one crew member she needed to find and thank personally. She took advantage of Torak being distracted by a council member reluctant to leave to glance around.

Her eyes narrowed on the crewman who had been aboard the Tearnat's warship and who had been talking to Torak before she had killed Trolis and fainted from exhaustion. She knew his name was Kev Mul Kar and he was Torak's Captain of the Guard. Seeing him standing to one side surveying the room she knew almost immediately when he felt her staring at him. Moving toward him, River let a small smile curve her lips.

"Captain Kar," River called out softly. "A moment of your time, please."

Kev Mul Kar watched as Torak's mate approached him. He knew what she wanted and flushed as she came closer. It was hard for him to ignore how beautiful she was. He had been fascinated with her when she had appeared on the Tearnat's ship, killing Progit and rescuing him and the others, but to see her dressed in the outfit she wore now, with her long hair braided down her back, and her unusual eyes highlighted even more by the dark coloring around them was almost more than his self control could handle. He was doing everything in his power not to make a fool of himself. Lady River had to be the most exotic, sensual creature he had ever seen, and her prowess as a warrior only added to her mystique.

Bowing his head slightly to acknowledge her position and his respect, Kev Mul Kar replied. "How may I serve you, my lady?"

River laughed. "By calling me River first."

Kev Mul Kar smiled back. "How may I serve you, Lady River?" he asked in a slightly husky voice.

"I wanted to thank you for retrieving my swords." River blushed a little before also apologizing. "I know I had no right to go into your room, but when I saw them I couldn't resist taking them. They mean a great deal to me," she added softly.

Kev Mul Kar looked into River's eyes, returning her smile. "They belong to you, Lady River. You have no need to apologize for taking what was rightfully yours."

"Nevertheless, thank you," River said, reaching up and giving Kev Mul Kar a hug.

Kev Mul Kar stood stiffly for a moment before he wrapped his arms around River's waist and returned her hug. He closed his eyes briefly as he felt her soft form, press against his harder one. Sensing sudden danger, he tensed.

Opening his eyes, his gaze met the deadly stare of Torak who stood frozen not twenty feet away. The intense cold gaze spoke of death if he did not release Torak's mate immediately. Reluctantly, Kev Mul Kar released his hold on River and stepped away, bowing briefly before turning and walking away. It was one of the hardest things he had ever done.

Chapter 8

Torak was silent on the shuttle ride down to the planet. River glanced at him from time to time, but mostly listened to the excited talk around her. The men were excited to finally be back home. Many of them had been away in space for almost a year, and were anxious to return to their Houses. Others talked about what had happened in the shuttle bay and how they had all held their breaths when River had issued her battle cry.

Jo and Star sat next to each other and between Manota and Jazin. Neither brother had let the sisters out of their sight since they had appeared in the shuttle bay. Jo looked at River and rolled her eyes, then crossed them and stuck her tongue out.

River bit back a laugh. She giggled when Torak looked at her before glancing up at Jo. His eyes narrowed as he watched the interaction between them. He said something to Jazin and Manota in a language that didn't translate in their translators. A moment later each man had a firm grip on his mate's wrist.

River raised an eyebrow at Torak when he looked down at her with a triumphant smirk. So, he thought speaking in a language that wasn't in the translator was fair? Well, turnabout was fair play.

Speaking in Cantonese, River explained her theory to Jo and Star watching the brothers' faces as she spoke. "I think they are trying something and don't want us to know about it."

All three brothers' heads swiveled around to look at River with a frown. Jo grinned and spoke in Italian. "I believe you are right. I don't think their translators work on a language other than English since it was the only one we spoke before."

Star watched as Jazin's face darkened; speaking in French, she added. "Well, if we mix up the languages they are never going to figure out what we are saying. Let's see if they like to eat crow as much as they like to dish it out."

River, Jo, and Star all laughed as the men scowled at them. Jazin muttered under his breath. "What did we do to deserve such females?" causing the girls to laugh even harder.

* * *

River was excited and scared at the same time as the shuttle landed. She loved to travel, but this was a little far out for her! She had not really had much time to absorb the fact she was on a spaceship traveling through space before, since she was more concerned with just trying to stay alive. Now, she was going to take her first step out onto an alien planet. Glancing at Jo and Star, River could tell they were just as nervous too.

Torak glanced down at River, watching as she nervously twisted a small knife between her fingers, moving it in and out without even looking at it. He had a feeling she wasn't even aware she was doing it since she kept looking around at everyone and everything.

Torak was very proud of his House as it was one of the largest and strongest on Kassis. He had made arrangements for a transport to take them to their House. The House of Kassis consisted of four main buildings.

The South building was made up of conference rooms, dining rooms, a medical wing, additional guest rooms for visiting dignitaries, and rooms for entertaining guests. The North wing was the Lead House, and it belonged to Torak. The Lead House housed the next leader of the House of Kassis and was Torak's primary residence now even though his father was still alive and the leader of Kassis.

His house consisted of his private armed security force and their families, his private quarters, the quarters of all those who were under his protection, additional guests' rooms for his private visitors, and numerous common living areas. The East House belonged to Manota and was known as the Second House of Kassis. It was built almost identical to the North House with only the few modifications Manota had done. It contained his personal security force, quarters for all those who were under his protection, and private and common living areas.

The last house was the West House, which belonged to Jazin, and was known as the Third House of Kassis. It was identical to the other two Houses. In the center between the Houses was a large garden area with fountains and paths leading to each of the three private Houses and the Common House. If necessary, the entire complex could be sealed off to become a giant fortress.

Torak looked forward to presenting River to his House. He had listened to his men talking about her entrance this morning and the challenge she had presented to Tai Tek. Each tale of her acts from rescuing them from a hideous death at the hands of Progit, to her knife throwing in the training room, to this morning's challenge to Tai Tek became even larger and grander than the one before.

If he were truthful to himself, he had to admit it was what happened after the councilmen had left that still bothered him and made him so possessive of keeping River close to him. When he had finally been able to get Councilman Rai Marcs to board his shuttle, he had been stunned to find River in the arms of his Captain of the Guard.

Fierce jealousy had swept through him at the sight of her wrapped in another warrior's arms. He had seen the tears glittering in her eyes as she stared up at Mul Kar, her arms wrapped around his neck, but even worse was the look on his Captain of the Guard's face. He had never seen emotion on the face of his most trusted guard before like he had at that moment. He knew it had taken everything in Mul Kar's power to pull back and walk away from River.

River glanced up startled when she felt Torak's hand tighten around her wrist suddenly. He was looking at her with a fierce glitter in his eyes, a look of pure determination and possession stamped on his face.

"Hey, you okay?" River asked softly, pulling gently on her wrist to let him know he was holding her a little tighter than she was expecting.

Torak's mouth drew into a firm line. "You are mine. You need to remember that."

River raised her eyebrow at him. What brought that on? "I thought we had cleared that up. I don't belong to anyone. I'm not something you can buy. I'm a human being who makes up her own mind," River whispered back fiercely.

"Well, make up your mind you belong to me," Torak replied before turning in his seat to show the discussion was over.

Of all the bull-headed, stubborn, arrogant, male-chauvinist— Ugh! River thought, leaning back against the seat. She glanced at Jo and Star who were staring at Torak and her. River crossed her eyes and signed to them he was driving her crazy. The sisters bit back a laugh nodding their heads in agreement.

* * *

River, Jo, and Star sat between the men exclaiming over all the different things they saw as the transport glided through the city. They had never seen a vehicle that traveled without the use of wheels except in the movies. After the shuttle had landed, they had been led to a huge vehicle about the size of a stretch limo but without a roof. It had been sitting about two feet off the ground with nothing holding it up.

Jo and Star had walked around and around the vehicle trying to see what was holding it up while River had actually gotten down on her hands and knees to look under it. The men had watched with humor as the girls made all kinds of excited exclamations about it. Torak had finally had to lift River bodily off the ground to seat her inside the transport so they could leave.

The rest of the ride had drawn some of the same types of reactions as the girls leaned over the men or stood up while the transport was moving to look at something they had just passed. If it hadn't been for the men's firm grips on the women they would have probably fallen out of the transport on more than one occasion as they swiveled to look at a building or any number of Kassisans walking along the roads.

The women drew almost as much attention as they sped through the city. Dressed as they were in the form fitting black sheaths, with their eyes highlighted, and their small figures, they caused more than one backup along the way. It appeared news had traveled fast about what had transpired on the *Galaxy Quest* this morning. Lines of people bordered the roadway trying to catch a glimpse of the three fierce female warrior women.

Torak shook his head as he had to grab for River yet again as she stood up and pointed at the statue of his father they had just passed.

"Little one, you must sit down before you fall out," Torak said as he pulled River onto his lap where he could wrap both of his arms around her.

"But, did you see that? It was like made of some type of crystal or something, and it glowed!" River said excitedly. Man, she wished her cell phone hadn't gone dead. She would be taking all kinds of pictures right now.

Torak laughed while his brothers chuckled at the sound of awe in River's voice. "Yes, it is made of a crystal we mine here on Kassis. You will see much of the crystal while you are here."

"Jo, you or Star don't have your cell phone or a camera, do you?" River asked as she twisted back and forth on Torak's lap.

Torak bit back a groan as he felt her sweet ass rubbing back and forth against his crotch. He could feel his cock swelling as she moved. It swelled in response to the innocent invitation she was unwittingly giving him.

He looked at his brothers who were biting back a laugh at his expense. They knew exactly what was happening to him and showed no sympathy at all for his discomfort. What amused them even more was the fact River was totally oblivious to her effect on Torak. The women of their Houses took great pleasure in trying to gain the attention of the men.

It was refreshing and extremely provocative to have three females who seemed unaware of their impact on the men. Not only were they unaware, they seemed to go out of their way to do just the opposite: they tried to drive the men away.

"Like, no," Star said sarcastically. "I seemed to have forgotten to pack it before I left for this little trip."

River just laughed. "Oops, sorry!"

Jo burst out laughing. All three girls leaned back as the entrance to the Houses of Kassis came into view. The Houses stood upon one of the highest levels of the city, giving each house a view of the city below.

"Wow! Talk about overkill," River breathed. Her head fell back against Torak as they passed under the elaborate gates leading to the front entrance.

Torak could not resist pressing a kiss into River's neck as she arched it to look back behind them without turning. He couldn't suppress the soft groan at her shivered reaction. River turned to look at Torak with a surprised expression. She looked into his eyes for a minute before blushing and turning to look as the Houses came closer.

That brief kiss fueled Torak's desire even more, causing his cock to grow even larger under her curvy ass. He heard River's quickly indrawn breath as she felt it. Torak pulled her even tighter into his lap when she would have moved away. He needed a moment to get himself under control before he let her go. Even then it was going to be obvious to anyone looking at his crotch how much of an effect River had on him.

Torak, Manota, and Jazin stood to one side of the transport watching carefully as the three females disembarked from it. Torak came up behind River, and laying his palm along the small of her back, guided her toward the entrance to the South House, explaining the purpose of each House.

"I live in the North House as the next leader of Kassis. You will live there with me," Torak said.

River bit back the retort she wanted to give him for his arrogant comment instead settling for a noncommittal reply. "We'll see."

Torak flashed an angry glance down at River before continuing through the foyer.

"My lords, welcome back," An elderly man said as he approached them. The man was dressed in some type of uniform with several medals hanging from his chest.

"Je'zi," came the response from each of the three brothers who walked up and gripped the elderly man's forearms.

"It is good to be home. All is well?" Torak asked, looking around.

"Yes, my lord. The House of Kassis had several visitors while you were away from the Eastern Regions. Your father met with them, and a new trade agreement was signed. I believe they are to return in several weeks to begin additional negotiations. The Lead House and the Second and Third Houses have been anxiously awaiting my lords' return," Je'zi finished, handing several documents to Torak before turning to hand additional ones to Manota and Jazin.

Once he had finished explaining what had been occurring during their absence, he added before leaving, "I will notify each House of your return, my lords."

River, Jo, and Star watched in amusement as the man turned sharply and walked out through two huge, elaborately carved doors. They had been gazing all around in amazement at the elaborate carvings, statues, and furnishings. Hell, even the walls and ceilings were over the top, and they had seen some really over-the-top places back on Earth. The ceiling seemed to glow with millions of little crystals. River was getting dizzy from turning round and round trying to take everything in.

The further they moved through the South House the more uneasy she felt. It was beautiful, but she didn't belong here. She was a simple girl by nature, enjoying the simple life of a traveling circus performer, not some grand lady. She'd visited places like this as a tourist, not lived in them.

By the time they had reached the gardens in the center between the four Houses, River had grown even quieter as the scale of the place Torak called home became more evident. She couldn't help, but admire the gardens as she gazed at the multitude of plants and flowers, marveling as they walked at the different combinations and how beautifully landscaped they were. Passing by even more fountains and statues made of crystal, she wrapped her arms around her waist to keep the shiver of depression from overwhelming her. There was no way she was going to be comfortable staying there.

She would have to talk with Jo and Star and see if they could find something smaller, just big enough for the three of them until they returned home. She could talk to Torak about it, too. Surely, he would know of a place. River was just going to broach the subject when Manota pulled Jo toward him and headed for the East House without a word of warning. Jazin quickly pulled Star toward him and the West House, ignoring her brief struggle. Both girls' protests died as the men swept them off their feet, not giving them time to argue.

River gazed after her friends feeling suddenly very alone and unsure. Torak placed his hand against her back again and gave her a gentle push toward his House. River moved slowly, wondering what she had gotten herself into.

* * *

The North House had huge curved steps leading to the front double doors which stood almost twenty feet high. River couldn't help but think movers wouldn't have any problems fitting furniture through doors that big before realizing what a stupid thought that was. As she moved into the foyer, she really wished she had her sunglasses to hide behind.

The closer they got to Torak's house the more people stopped and stared at her. She didn't mind it when she was performing, but River was very shy outside the ring. Since she couldn't hide behind dark glasses, she took to keeping her gaze down so she didn't have to see the people staring at her. It was only when she heard a cry go up that she raised her eyes to see what all the fuss was about.

River couldn't believe her eyes as she and Torak stepped into the foyer of the North House. Women poured out of rooms, down stairs, and through the doors to surround Torak—kissing him all over, running their hands over his body, and saying all kinds of things that made River blush furiously.

She had never heard women talk like that, not even in the movies. Torak just stood there smiling at the women, letting them kiss and pet him as if he was some type of forgotten favorite pet just rediscovered. The icing on the cake came when a tall, thin woman several years older than River came down the stairs wearing a beautiful but very skimpy gown.

The gown itself was practically see-through and the top, what there was of it, didn't even cover all of her nipples. River gawked for a minute before turning to stare at Torak. He just smiled as the tall woman came to him and pulled his head down for a deep kiss.

River felt sick to her stomach as she watched the woman run her hands over Torak's body as she pressed herself into him. Unable to stomach any more, River turned on her heel and walked out the front doors, which were still stood open, and down the steps.

"Oh, my lord, I have missed you greatly," Javonna said huskily.

She had heard Torak was back and had prepared carefully for his return wearing a gown she knew would entice him to her bed. Pressing herself against him, she let him feel her nipples as they swelled at the thought of him loving them.

Torak smiled down on Javonna as he gently pulled her arms from around his neck. She had been one of his frequent lovers in his House, and he had enjoyed her very much for a time. But now that he had River he found he did not like her touching him.

She smelled overwhelmingly of a flowered perfume, and her curves did not feel as soft as River's did in his arms. Even though she was experienced in knowing how to bring a man to the height of arousal, he found he had no desire for her.

Pulling her arms down and holding them so she could not wrap them around his neck again, Torak said loudly. "I would like to present, Lady River, my mate, Head of the House of Kassis, and future mother to the heirs of Kassis."

Torak turned to look at the place where he had left River standing when he had entered his House to be greeted. He thought she would be highly impressed with the number of females under his protection as it showed he was a very powerful man to have so many. Instead, she was nowhere to be seen. Twirling around to scan the room, he called out for her only to get no response.

* * *

River was beyond furious. She was mortified and humiliated. She angrily wiped at the tears spilling down her face.

That arrogant man-whore. That—that slimy weasel. That... she was so mad she couldn't even think of any more bad things to call him. *That jerk!* She thought with a nod.

She had never been so shocked or hurt in all her life. To think he told her she was his. Fat lot that meant! Torak must have had over twenty women pawing all over him and that—that one woman wasn't even dressed!

Practically running now, she paused in the center of the garden unsure of which way to go...Star or Jo. It was only when she rounded the center fountain that she saw Jo sitting on the edge of it holding a crying Star.

"What happened?" River asked as she came around the fountain to kneel in front of the two sisters. She could tell Jo had been crying too.

"Those— Those—" Jo choked on her rage. "Assholes!" She practically screamed her frustration at not finding a better word to call them.

"You too?" River asked.

Star pulled away to look at River, tears streaming down her puffy cheeks. "Jazin must have had a hundred women pawing at him! When he asked me why I was upset as they were trying to take his clothes off him right in front of me, I lost it. I called him a gigolo and took off running."

Jo looked at River. "Same here, only I decked him when he tried to kiss me after all those other women had kissed him. Like I really wanted to taste them on him!" Jo said bitterly.

River nodded, sitting next to the sisters. "Torak had about twenty women pawing at him. One of the women was wearing this see-through number with her nipples showing. I just walked out while she was shoving her tongue down his throat," River sniffed.

Jo looked at Star and River with determination. "I want to go home. To Earth. Today wouldn't be too soon as far as I'm concerned. At least there I know what assholes guys can be sometimes. Here it seems to be the norm."

River and Star both nodded in agreement. This helped them see the decision they had been reluctant to make. It was time to go home to Earth. They did not belong here, in this world. River stood up, putting her hand out. The other two looked at it for a minute before putting theirs on top in a show of solidarity.

..*

Torak was frantic. He met his brothers as they ran down the paths toward his House.

"Have you seen Star?" Jazin asked frantically, looking at Torak. "She took off."

"So did Jo," Manota said. His left eye puffed out a little.

Torak looked at Manota, startled. "What happened to you?"

"Jo punched me when I tried to kiss her," Manota said in confusion. "She was very upset about something, but she wouldn't tell me what it was."

Jazin looked at Torak and Manota. "My Star was very upset, also. She called me a 'gigolo'—whatever that means—and took off before I could stop her."

"Where is River?" Jazin and Manota asked at the same time.

Torak ran his hand down over his neck. "I don't know. One minute she was there, the next she was gone. I was going to introduce her to my House, but she had disappeared. Why would all three of them be so upset?" Torak asked, confused, looking from one brother to the other.

"Jazin, what were you doing right before Star left?" Torak asked.

"I was being greeted by my House," Jazin replied, puzzled.

"What about you, Manota?" Torak asked.

"The same. The females of my House were welcoming me home. Nothing unusual," Manota said, before adding, "Except for when Jo punched me."

"What about you? What were you doing?" Manota asked.

"I was being greeted by the females of my House as is the custom upon our return. Nothing that should have upset River," Torak said.

"We better find them before they find each other. We know what happens when they get together," Jazin said.

* * *

River, Jo, and Star decided they would work their way back to where the shuttle had landed. From there they would hijack one of the shuttles, forcing someone to take them to the warship, if they had to. That was as far as they had gotten by the time the men found them.

River twirled around, pulling her swords out and pointing them at Torak as he, Manota, and Jazin came into view.

"Stay back, you... you... jerk," she snarled.

She had worked her way through the shock of seeing him being pawed on to pure fury. Jo and Star each took up a stance keeping the men in their sights.

They were just as worked up as River was and more than ready to clobber someone.

"River, little one, tell me why you are so upset," Torak pleaded softly.

"Upset? You think I'm upset?" River screeched. All three men cringed as her voice broke on the high note.

"Star, baby. Please come back to my House," Jazin said, stepping toward Star.

Star's eyes narrowed. "When hell freezes over you... you slut! I wouldn't go back to your House for all the money in the world!"

"Jo, put down your weapon now," Manota demanded. "You will return with me to my House where we can discuss why you are so upset."

Jo looked at Manota and gave him an ugly smile. "Over your dead body," she replied coolly.

Torak could see the females had already spent time together which meant they had banded together on whatever they had decided. It was not going to be easy separating them again. In fact, if the looks on their faces were to be believed, it would be damn near impossible.

River coolly looked at Torak. "You promised you would return us to our home if we released you. I am calling in that promise."

Torak's eyes turned cold at River's demand. "I promised to take you home and I have. Your home is here now."

River pulled her sword up pointing it at Torak's neck. "That was not the deal. The deal was to return us to our home, Earth. This is not our home, and it never will be. Either you return us, or we will find a way on our own."

Torak stepped into the blade River had pointed at his throat, letting the sharp edge cut a small, thin line along his throat. "I have claimed you as mine, River. Your home is now on Kassis. I will never let you go, and I will kill anyone who tries to help you or take you from me," Torak said in a cold, steely voice.

River's eyes widened as she watched a small line of blood form from the cut. "Then I'll die trying to get away from you because I will never belong to you. Never!" River replied shakily.

River shivered as she watched the cold look settle over Torak's face. She had never seen him look like that before, not even when Progit threatened to kill his brother. He looked like he would do whatever had to be done to keep her.

River was staring into Torak's eyes, trying to decide what to do next when she saw a flash out of the corner of her eye. Her gaze flicked over to the flash, and her eyes widened in horror. She cried out as she tossed one sword to the side and pushed Torak away, knocking him to the ground when she hooked her foot in between his legs and shoved his shoulder.

Torak cursed as he fell to the ground. He had been furious at River's refusal to accept his claim on her and her insistence he return her to her planet. When she had said she would rather die than belong to him, he had become overwhelmed with fury. How dare she deny him! He was the next leader of his planet, the ruler of his House, and she would rather die than be with him! He could tell she was trying to think of a way to get out of the situation when her eyes had suddenly widened in horror. Before he could respond, she had dropped her sword and pushed him to the ground.

Jo turned as something sprayed her cheek. She had been too busy glaring at Manota to pay attention to what was going on around her. She knew River was arguing with Torak about taking them home, then the next minute she was yelling, "Watch out!" to everyone.

Jo raised her hand to wipe at the liquid running down her cheek. She let out a small scream when she looked down at her hand and noticed the liquid was, in fact, blood. Manota realized what it was at the same time Jazin did. Both men grabbed the sisters and pulled them down to the ground behind the fountain.

River remained standing, looking down at Torak in disbelief. Torak lay on the ground, looking up at her, his expression changing from fury to horror as she pulled her hand away from her chest to look at the blood soaking the front of her shirt. Just as quickly, she crumpled to the ground next to him.

Chapter 9

Torak let out a roar for his security guards even as he rolled to shield River's body. River lay on her side, her blood soaking into the pebbled path. She was having trouble breathing, and everything was beginning to get fuzzy around the edges. Her breaths came in shallow gasps as she tried to suck in enough oxygen to speak.

Torak rolled River over onto her back to see how badly she was injured. He could tell from her breathing and the amount of blood it had to be very bad. Ripping his shirt off, he grabbed the front of River's shirt and tore the front open, exposing the sports bra she liked to wear.

She had a small entry wound in her upper chest. From the amount of blood pooling under her the shot had gone through her body, exiting out the back. Torak's hands shook as he tore his shirt in half trying to staunch the flow of blood from the wound. All around him there were shouts as members from each House's elite guard went into action. Within moments, a team of healers was pulling at each of them, checking for injuries.

Torak knocked the hands reaching for him away, instead yelling for the healer to take care of River. He watched as the healer quickly yelled out instructions and an anti-gravity MED-bed was brought closer. He stared into River's eyes, watching as she fought for breath; silent tears coursed down from the corner of her eyes before she closed them.

"*No!*" Torak roared out, fighting the hands gripping him.

"*No!*" he yelled again hoarsely, never taking his eyes off River's pale, still face.

"Torak, come. We must get under cover," Manota said desperately. He had to get his brothers and Jo and her sister to safety.

"Come. They will bring her to medical," Manota said forcefully, pulling on Torak.

Torak fought as Jazin and Manota pulled him away from River. He twisted around just in time to see a healer straddle River's body and force air into her. Other healers were working to get the needed equipment in place to transport her.

"The healers are doing all they can to save her. Come, we must get the other two females to safety," Manota said again.

Torak's Captain of the Guard, Kev Mul Kar, had several of his men escorting the two women toward the Common House. Manota was frantic to make sure the blood on Jo was not hers. Both women moved quickly into the Common House, following the men to the medical wing. Not long after they had arrived one of the healers came out to check on Jo and Star.

"What of the other female, my mate Lady River?" Torak asked anxiously.

"The other healers are trying to stabilize her as we speak," the healer said, looking with sympathy at Torak. "It does not look good. I will inform you of her condition once they have evaluated her," the healer added before leaving the room, satisfied neither Jo nor Star was injured.

Jo and Star had cried until they couldn't cry any more as they waited to hear if River was going to make it. Shortly after the healer had left, he came back again, calling out to Torak. The healer said they had River stable for the time being, but that she had lost too much blood.

She had sustained injuries to her internal organs, including a nick to one of the valves in her heart. They were not sure if the blood they had would be compatible and were hesitant to use it on her with her being so weak. Jo and Star knew they shared the same blood type as River and had volunteered to donate what they could.

Now, they sat quietly, sipping a sweetened fruit juice of some type, feeling very tired. The stress of arriving at the Houses to find the men they had been falling in love with surrounded by eager females, River's getting shot, and donating more blood than they should have had left them weak.

Torak brushed off Javonna's hand again as he paced back and forth. Unable to deal with her touch, he finally ordered her back to the North House. Javonna had been very unhappy about Torak's refusal to return with her. Jo and Star just watched Torak with disgust.

"I don't even know why you are even here," Jo said coldly to Torak. "Haven't you done enough to River without causing her more pain and humiliation?"

Torak turned to stare at Jo. Taking a menacing step toward her, he gritted out through clenched teeth. "Watch what you say. Warrior woman or not, I am in no mood for your ridicule."

Manota walked over to stand closer to Jo, putting his hand on her shoulder. He flinched when she stood up, moving further away from him. "Keep your filthy hands to yourself."

"Why are you so angry?" Jazin asked softly. "What have we done that had caused all three of you to suddenly hate us?"

Star looked at Jazin, tears filling her eyes. "You really don't know?"

Jazin just shook his head, his heart breaking at the look of utter devastation on Star's small face.

"It's all the women you have," Jo replied harshly. "You may not mind having a harem of women pawing all over you but we do. We don't share. Ever," Jo couldn't keep the tears from her own eyes any longer so she turned her back on Manota.

All three men stood frozen. They'd had no idea this was what had upset River, Jo, and Star so much. It was an accepted practice on Kassis for a House to have many, many females in them. In fact, the more women there were, the more prominence the House was considered to have since it took a strong warrior to satisfy so many women. The male would not breed with any of the females in the House except for the one he claimed as a mate. Since the males were so sexually active it was accepted by his mate that he would keep other females so as to not distress his mate with his overactive sexual desires. Now, these warrior women were telling them it was because of this practice they did not want anything to do with them.

"I do not understand," Torak replied, looking back and forth between Jo and Star. "Your males do not have more than one female in their House?"

Jo took a deep breath, shaking her head before turning around and looking Torak in the eye. "No. Not if they want to live or at least not lose any body parts they are fond of."

Jo walked back over and sat next to Star, motioning for the three men to sit as well. Only after all three men were seated did Jo and Star begin explaining how relationships on Earth evolved.

"On Earth, it is the norm to have one male and one female. They usually love each other very much and are committed to building a life together. If it is a good relationship, they are monogamous, meaning they never touch another male or female in a sexual way again. There are names on our planet for the way you guys have relationships and none of them are very nice. River, Star, and I are into only having one man in our lives who is devoted only to the one of us he is with. If that man was to ever, and I mean *ever*, have a sexual encounter of any type with another female, or male, then the relationship would be over, and we would be gone so fast he wouldn't know what hit him," Jo said looking at Manota.

"But, how is the male's strength known if he does not have but one female?" Jazin asked looking at Star.

"Trust me when I say, one female is all he needs," Star responded. "Let me ask you this. How would you have felt today if you had walked into my House, as you put it, and I had as many guys kissing and touching me as you had women?"

All three men paled at the idea of so many males touching and feeling on their woman. Flushing a dark red, Jazin replied hotly, "I would kill them all!"

"Well, that is precisely how we felt," Jo replied. "By the way, you know a woman can handle more than one guy at a time a lot better than one guy can handle more than one woman. Not to mention a woman is capable of having multiple orgasms where a guy is good for one shot, even if it only takes him a little while to recharge," Jo said stiffly.

"How would you know?" Manota said, standing up and glowering down at Jo.

"Books, movies, the Internet," Jo added hastily. "Not from personal experience."

"So you are saying River left me because of the women in my House. She... all of you... want to return to your world because of the women we have in our Houses?" Torak asked, trying to understand what Jo and Star were telling him and his brothers.

"Yes," came the soft reply from both girls.

"I can tell you no matter what any of you do, as long as you have the women you have been fucking living under the same roof as you are, none of us will stay. Ever," Star said, looking into Jazin's eyes.

"Even then, I think it is going to be hard to forget," Jo added, glancing at Manota before turning away from him, but not before he had seen the pain and betrayal in her eyes and the tremble to her lip.

"I can tell you now, Torak. If that woman who was here a little while ago is anywhere near River when she wakes up, I'll kill her and you myself," Star said, looking into Torak's eyes to let him know she meant it. "I won't let you or anyone else hurt River. She doesn't deserve it and neither do we."

Torak nodded. He had a lot to think about. His biggest fear, he suddenly realized, was he wouldn't be given the chance to prove to River how much he loved her. Shaken by his realization that River meant so much to him, he sank back into his chair, staring blindly toward the door of the waiting room.

Chapter 10

Torak was ready to go out of his mind. None of the healers had come back since they had taken Jo and Star to donate blood. It had been almost twelve hours since River had been shot.

Torak paced back and forth ready to charge back into the medical unit to find River. The others had finally given up and found a place to sleep. Star was asleep with her head on Jazin's lap on the couch while Jo was curled up on Manota's lap. She had fallen asleep sitting in the chair and only after she had done so had Manota picked her up. She still wasn't talking to him unless she had to, and she refused to look at him for any length of time. Torak jerked around, and both girls sat up with a start when the door opened.

An elderly healer walked into the room looking exhausted. His face was pale and drawn as he looked around the room at the faces looking at him with so much hope.

Turning his gaze to Torak, he let out a tired sigh. "My lord, your mate should survive," he said tiredly. "It was very close, and she is not entirely out of danger."

"Why is she still in danger? Our soldiers have suffered worse wounds and not taken so long to heal. Why is she still suffering?" Torak demanded.

The healer looked at Torak before replying. "There is much more to healing than just the body. There is the mind as well. Your mate had made the decision it was her time to go to the next life."

Torak fell back as what the healer told him sank in. "But why? How can you know this?" he whispered.

Jo pulled away from Manota and hurried over to the couch where Star sat holding herself tightly, trying not to cry again.

"She loves you," Star whispered. "She has almost from the very beginning."

Torak sank into the chair by the window, staring at Star. "River told this to you?"

Star looked at Torak before answering him. "River has never felt comfortable around the opposite sex. You are the only one she has ever let near her. Oh, she went out on a date or two, but she never got serious with anyone. Not even Billy Myers and she actually went out on two dates with him. It's not just that; I knew when we were in the vents. She would sneak off to go find you and be gone for hours. She was watching you, making sure you were okay. She worried about you."

"And, don't forget what happened yesterday," Jo continued. "She saw you were in danger and protected you even at the risk of her own life. Even hurt by what to us is a deep betrayal, she couldn't stand that you were in danger."

The healer listened quietly before adding, "I believe the young ladies are correct. Lady River asked that I convey to you a message should she not survive before she became unconscious. She wanted me to tell you that she hoped you found happiness, my lord."

Torak looked at the healer in shock. "You said she should survive, not that she will. What needs to be done to make sure she will survive?"

"I believe only you have the power to give her the will to do so, my lord," the healer replied before bowing his head in respect and leaving the room.

"What should I do?" Torak looked at his brothers. For the first time, he felt at a loss as to how to take command of a situation. There was too much to lose if he should make the wrong decision.

Jo stood up and put her hands on her hips before glaring at all three men. "Well, for starters, you can get rid of all the women in your Houses! I can guarantee you none of us will be setting foot into any of those Houses ever again as long as one female you've fucked is still there, not to mention you won't be touching us."

Star stood up and nodded her agreement, looking at Jazin as she did. "That goes for all of us. Come on, Jo, let's go find River and sit with her."

The three brothers watched as two out of the three women they loved walked out the door. All three of them had some changes to make in their Houses if they were going to keep the alien warrior women who had struck a blow to their hearts and souls.

* * *

"Do you remember the time Jenny the Juggler and Mad Andy got into it?" Star was saying as Torak came into the room where River was lying so pale and still. "Jenny started tossing his pigeons at him, and he was running around in circles not knowing what to do, trying to catch the damn things. It was the funniest thing until he ran into the pole when he wasn't looking and knocked himself out. Poor Jenny cried for a week every time she saw his face after that. No one had the heart to tell her he had already broken his nose on more than one occasion, so it wasn't her fault it was so crooked."

Jo laughed. "Yeah, and remember the time the monkeys got loose and stole the clowns' cars? They drove them all around the rink, running over Walter's foot, and knocking poor Marcus into the tank he was filling up with water."

Torak frowned as the girls told one story after another about people called Jeffrey the Snakeman or Donna the Dragonbreather. It was only when they started talking about some of the things River had done that he stopped them to ask questions.

"You said Marcus the Magnificent cut River in half and refused to put her back together again until she told him where his rabbits were? How could she have lived through something like that?" Torak asked, looking back and forth between the two women.

Followed by, "What is a rabbit?"

"Why did she hide them?

"Who is Walter?"

"Why did she battle the clowns?"

"What is a clown?" Was the last straw for the girls. Their laughter rang through the room.

"Will you please keep it down? There's a girl trying to get her beauty sleep here," River murmured faintly.

"River?" Jo and Star said, at the same time reaching for her hand.

River had a hard time forcing her eyelids to lift. She had been listening to Jo and Star reminiscing for the past twenty minutes or so, enjoying the cadence of their voices and the happy memories they had been talking about. She had been about to open her eyes when another voice had spoken softly. Torak.

River had felt tears gather in her eyes as she remembered him wrapped in the tall, slim woman's embrace. She didn't have the strength to fight him right now. She had hoped he would leave, but instead he had begun asking questions about things that were important to her, things that had made her happy.

River opened her eyes and stared above Jo's and Star's heads, gazing into Torak's beautiful, dark eyes. "A clown is someone who can make you laugh, even when you are hurting," River replied softly, tears glistening in her eyes and spilling over to splash down her cheek.

"Then I need to find these clowns and bring them to you," Torak said softly.

Jo and Star looked back and forth between Torak and River. Jo stood, motioning for Star to follow her. Star stopped as she moved past Torak.

"Remember what I told you. I meant it," she said before she blew River a kiss and left her alone with Torak.

River stared at Torak for several minutes before her gaze dropped to the covers lying over her. "What did she tell you?"

"That if I hurt you again she would kill me," Torak replied.

River's eyes flew up to Torak's before she lowered them again, biting her lip to keep the small smile from escaping at the idea of little, gentle Star killing a warrior over twice as big as her.

"She'd do it too," River couldn't help but say.

Torak walked over to River, gently picking up her hand before sitting on the bed next to her. "I know. And, I would let her," he added.

River looked at Torak and shook her head. "I can't go back there. I won't," River's lip trembled and she raised a shaking hand to wipe away a stray tear.

"We will talk about that later. You are still weak," Torak gazed down into River's pale face, brushing her hair away from it.

He had never seen her hair down until a few days ago when Jo and Star had undone the braid to wash her hair. When he had walked in they had been talking like they were today, like she was really there with them. They had just finished bathing her and had dressed her in a new gown. He had walked in as they were holding her gently, brushing her long, dark hair until it shone like delicate dew on the webs of the thread trees.

It had been over a week since she had been shot, but she had still not awakened. The healer had been right. They had been able to heal her body, but not her mind. She had retreated from the world of the living into the shadow world of a half-life, her body here but her mind there. Jo and Star had called it a coma. They said that on their planet, it was believed if someone was in a coma, they could still hear those who were in the land of the living, and it was important to talk to the person so they could find their way back.

During the day, Jo and Star had remained at River's side while Manota, Jazin, and he had taken care of business within their Houses. Any and all females whom they had had as a lover were no longer there. The only females that remained were those who were mated, young children, or elderly women. It had not been an easy task, as many of the females fought their transfer to another House.

In Torak's House, Javonna had been the most difficult, screaming, cursing, and finally threatening River's life. It was only when she made that final statement that Torak had enough. The threat against River was too much considering she was fighting for her life as Javonna spoke of ending it.

Torak had threatened to have her put to death for the threat and Mul Kar would have been only too eager to carry out the death sentence. Torak had noticed his Captain of the Guard was keeping close tabs on River's condition and had even visited her on one occasion, though never alone. Torak knew any and everything that touched River's life now. Never again would she be threatened or harmed if he could prevent it.

Nighttime was the time he spent with River. In the stillness of the night he would read to her, tell her stories of when he and his brothers were young, talk about his people, and brush her long hair, telling her how much he loved her and needed her. He didn't know if she heard him or not, but it had been a time of healing for himself.

He found, for the first time in his life, he wanted to know more about someone other than his men or his brothers. He wanted to know more about River. What her favorite color was, what she like to eat, what she did for relaxation, what type of stories she was interested in. In short, he wanted to know everything there was to know about her.

River was too tired to fight so she just nodded her head. "What happened? I know Jo and Star are all right, but what about your brothers?"

Torak picked up the brush from the side table and carefully helped River into a sitting position. Her shoulders felt so small and fragile. It felt as if a soft breeze might blow her away.

Torak gripped the brush tightly as he thought about how close he had been too losing her forever. Taking a deep breath to drive the pain away, he slid behind her on the bed, pulling her so she was between his legs and leaning back against him. He began brushing her hair gently as he spoke.

"They are fine. Kev found some shell casings on the roof of the South House. The casings belong to a commonly used weapon preferred by assassins." Torak murmured as he brushed her hair.

River tried to turn around, but she couldn't as she was trapped between Torak's arms and legs. "Why would anyone want to assassinate you?"

"I am the next leader of Kassis and head of the House of Kassis. There are many who are unhappy that our house supported the end of the war," he responded quietly.

"So you will always be in danger?" River asked with a shiver. It seemed like it didn't matter what world you lived in; if you were powerful, you were in danger.

"Most of the time I am very safe. Our security forces are the best in the galaxy, and I am very difficult to kill," Torak murmured as he pressed a kiss into the side of River's neck where he had pulled her hair back.

River shivered, and she felt her womb clench at the feel of his lips. Oh, but she wanted to feel his lips on her. Tilting her head to the side to expose more of her neck, she laid her head on his shoulder.

"Ah, little one, you are so beautiful. My beautiful warrior woman," Torak said as he laid the brush down on the bed and wrapped his hands around her stomach, sliding them further up until they rested under her breasts.

River moaned as she relaxed back into Torak enjoying the feel of his strong arms wrapped around her. When he moved them up so the weight of her breasts rested in his palms River thought she would come right there. Never in her life had she felt so fragile, so beautiful, so loved. She could feel Torak's hard cock pulsing against her back telling her he was not immune to what was happening.

"Torak," River whispered laying her hands over his and guiding them up until they covered her breasts.

Torak groaned as he felt her nipples pebble in the palms of his hands. Pulling and pinching them through the soft, thin material he rocked his hips against River.

River's breath was coming in small pants as Torak rolled her nipples between his fingers and the material of her gown. He pinched them just hard enough that River jumped, leaning forward. Torak took advantage to scoot further under River so she was sitting on his lap, his cock pressed against her pussy. The only thing between his cock and her pussy was the thin material of his pants and her gown.

"Oh Torak," River moaned, rubbing her pussy on his hard length.

"Sit back, River. Lie on me," Torak whispered hoarsely. He might not be able to seek relief for himself, but he could give her relief.

River trembled as she lay back against Torak's broad chest. She felt him gather the material of her gown in his hand and slide it up until he could touch the soft, downy curls between her legs. River jerked back as he used the fingers on one of his hands to spread her soft lips. River cried out as he rubbed his finger over her clit. She had never felt anything like this before. Her body was burning, and she could feel the moisture seeping from between her legs as he rubbed her clit. River began to shake as he slid his other hand around her, pulling her even closer so he could pull her lips apart with one hand while rubbing her swollen nub with the other. River let her head drop back against Torak as he moved his finger back and forth changing positions and speed.

"Beautiful," Torak murmured, looking down and watching as he stroked River's clit. "Watch what I am doing, little one. Watch while I bring you pleasure."

River's eyes moved down to watch what Torak was doing to her. She watched as he parted her lips. Her eyes grew wide as she watched him stroke her clit, rubbing it back and forth. The shaking in her body increased, and she cried out her climax while she watched his fingers disappear inside her to pump and stroke her. She tried to lean forward to get away from the overwhelming feelings as he continued to pull the orgasm out of her, drawing it out until it became too much, and she collapsed against him sobbing.

Torak slowly pulled his fingers out of River, letting them slide over her ultra-sensitive nub. River jerked as Torak ran his fingers over her. He slowly pulled her gown back down over her and pulled her closer to him, burying his face in her hair. He could smell her arousal, and he fought hard not to react to it.

His body was throbbing painfully with desire. Never before had he considered the pleasure of another person over his own. Now, he could not imagine only taking his pleasure and never fulfilling hers. She had been wild in his hands. He could tell she was an innocent to what had just happened. She had not used any of the wails other women with more experience used. If he was not mistaken, she had not even known what was happening until the orgasm was upon her.

Torak held River in his arms until he felt sure she had fallen back asleep. In a few days he would take her to his House. Tomorrow, he would begin the process of wooing her as Jo and Star had said he needed to do if he was to win back her trust.

He knew he already had her love. She might not be ready to admit it, but he had seen it shining from her eyes as she had stared at him after she had been shot. He would bide his time until she was ready to admit it. Only then could he claim her as his own.

Chapter 11

River had been waiting nervously for Torak to appear. Jo and Star had come over early this morning to help her get ready. She was still weak from having lost so much blood and from being in a coma for almost two weeks but was getting stronger every day. She had blushed at first when they insisted on helping her in the shower until they told her they had bathed her while she was unconscious. They had helped her dress and brushed out her long hair, fixing it on top of her head in an elaborate up-sweep.

The only time River had protested was when they had helped her dress. She had been surprised when they had walked in wearing long gowns. Jo had explained they were trying to compromise with the men and had decided they would try the gowns on a temporary basis.

Star had already decided they were going to make some alterations to the gowns so they were really pants made to look like dresses. They had brought a beautiful dark, blue gown that matched River's eyes. The gown fitted her willowy figure like a second skin, pushing up her breasts and showing off her delicate features.

After they had helped her stand in front of the mirror, River had blushed at her appearance. She had never felt so feminine in her whole life. With her dark hair piled up on her head and her dark blue eyes outlined with black liner she looked as far from a warrior as you could get.

"I even made a few quick adjustments on your gown," Star said, smiling as she pulled out a small bag containing six knives. There were four small knives and two larger ones.

"I thought the smaller ones would fit around your waist and blend in with the belt. The two larger knives are strapped to you, one on your thigh, which has a small zipper type opening to reach it and one on the inside of your arm with the same type of opening so no one would know about them unless they use a metal detector," Star said as she slipped the knives into their sheaths.

River's eyes glistened with tears as she stared at Star. "You are the best sister in the whole universe."

"Now, no crying," Jo muttered. "If you do, you'll ruin all my hard work."

"Okay, no crying," River laughed.

Her breath suddenly caught in her throat as she looked up to see Torak standing in the door staring at her. She blushed a bright pink when she thought about what he had done to her body a few days earlier. Turning slowly, River glanced nervously at Torak, playing with the skirt of her gown.

"Hi," River said shyly.

"You are beautiful, little one," Torak said huskily. He couldn't take his eyes off her. She was breathtaking.

Jo and Star grinned. "Well, thankfully you don't have too far to go. We'll see you later this evening, River."

"But…" River said, panicking, but it was too late. Both Jo and Star had already disappeared out the door in a fit of giggles.

River gazed at Torak again and blushed even redder. "I don't know where to go," she said in a small voice.

She turned her gaze down to the floor. She had been staying in the Medical Wing since the day she had arrived on Kassis. She wasn't sure what was going to happen to her now.

Torak moved quietly toward River. Placing his fingers under her chin, he lifted it until he could look into her eyes. "You will join me in my House."

He put his finger on her lips when she started to protest. "You will be the only female there I will look at. All others are either mated, very young, or elderly. There are no others, River. Only you."

River felt tears burn her eyes as she remembered the last time she had been in his house. She was afraid to trust what he was telling her. Torak could see the indecision in her eyes. He could tell she was afraid to trust him.

Bending down, he captured her lips as he pulled her closer to his body. He felt River's body relax into his and took advantage of her acceptance by running his hand down her body to cup her ass. He felt her mouth open, and he plunged his tongue into it, making love to her mouth with the same intensity, the same love as he had her pussy the other day. By the time he released her, she had melted into his arms.

Torak swept River off her feet as he felt her knees give way. He was beginning to enjoy this wooing. He was harder than hell, but he was more interested in her enjoyment than his own fulfillment.

Over the past several days he had learned more about River. He knew she loved the color blue, was afraid of spiders, whatever those were, was picky about who touched her knives, had been given her short battle swords as a sixteenth birthday present from her parents, and enjoyed listening to a variety of music. He had spent every free minute he could with River each day, falling more in love her as he discovered she was just as beautiful on the inside as she was on the outside.

Pulling her closer to his body, he couldn't wait until he had her in his bed tonight. He was going to know every nook, every line, every dimple on her body by the time he took his own pleasure.

Striding out the door of the medical wing, he didn't even pause as River said a breathless thank you to the healer as they passed him. The elderly healer just chuckled as he watched the lord of Kassis carry his mate to his House. He would not be at all surprised if there was a new heir within the year. Whistling under his breath the healer walked down the corridor with a new spring to his step.

˙

River raised her face to the bright sun as Torak carried her out of the South House and down the steps into the gardens. She looked around cautiously as he moved further into the gardens.

"Do you think it is safe to be out here?" River asked nervously.

"Yes, little one. A force field had been in place ever since you were shot. No one enters or leaves the House of Kassis without us knowing about it. To enter, I, one of my brothers, or my father must give permission or whoever enters will be incapacitated until given an antidote." Torak explained in a calm voice.

"How is that possible?" River asked astonished. She had only heard of stuff like that on the Sci-Fi Channel at home.

"Everyone entering must give a blood sample and be approved. A thorough search is done on anyone entering." Torak said with a reassuring smile.

"But, what about unexpected visitors?" River asked curiously.

"They can enter parts of the South House, where all guests will be housed until further notice. The security grid is very precise," Torak said, looking amused at all of River's questions.

"Well, what about if they wanted to come from up there?" River asked pointing straight up toward the sky.

"You cannot see it, but the force field completely covers this entire area. It is meant to not be seen," Torak replied smugly.

"Wow," was all River said. She couldn't think of any more questions. Instead, she looked around curiously, wondering where Torak was taking her.

Torak had turned down a path leading off to the side of his House. River laid her head on his shoulder, enjoying the feel of his warm body and tight arms. She had been afraid she would be too heavy for him to carry her any distance, but so far he didn't act tired at all, and she was enjoying being carried too much to suggest walking.

It wasn't until he moved under a canopy of trees that she gasped in surprise. On the other side of the tree was a small pond with flowers and some type of colorful bird swimming in it. Near the bank was a blanket and a small basket. Torak walked over to the blanket and gently laid River down onto it.

"I thought you might like to be outside for a little while after being cooped up on the warship for so long and then the medical wing," Torak said as he sat next to her.

River stared up at Torak. She couldn't believe he was being so thoughtful. The last few days had been wonderful. He had spent time with her—just talking, though she had hoped for more. River nervously licked her lips as she remembered what he had done to her. She remembered the feel of his hands on her, the way his fingers moved over and then in her.

Torak groaned as he watched River. "Little one, you stretch the limits of my control. I am trying to behave myself. I had not planned on making love to you until later."

River looked at Torak with desire-laden eyes. "You plan on making love to me later?" she asked, staring at his lips.

"Yes. Now behave or all my good intentions will be for nothing. Would you like something to eat?" Torak said, trying desperately to distract River.

He could feel her desire, and it was playing hell with all his good intentions. He had planned on talking with her, learning more about her home world while they ate, then possibly giving her a few chaste kisses while he learned even more about her, then letting her sleep for a little while. He had planned everything out carefully.

And all of it went out the window when River suddenly launched herself into his arms, closing her lips over his and knocking him backward. River grabbed Torak's cheeks, nipping at his lips and taking advantage of his mouth when he opened it. River's tongue slid in between his lips, teasing and taunting Torak's until he groaned and returned her kiss. When Torak's tongue fought back and slid into River's, she clamped down, sucking on it. Torak almost came apart when River began her innocent sucking up and down along his tongue as if it was his cock she was sucking. The image was burned into his brain, and all he could do was hang on to the fragile threads of his control which were breaking and shattering at an appalling rate.

Turning over until he had River under him, he slid between her legs, hoping to trap her body for a moment until he could get back under control.

"River. River, we have… to stop… now… or I cannot… promise… you I will," Torak said between kisses. River was kissing him every couple of words, making it almost impossible to get a sentence out.

"Don't... want... to," River whispered back.

River grabbed the leather tie that held Torak's hair back, pulling it loose until his hair fell forward.

"So beautiful," River whispered. "Just like you."

River leaned up and kissed Torak deeply, wrapping her arms around his neck and running her hands through his hair, scraping his scalp with her nails.

Torak gave up trying to resist her. He had wanted her from the moment he had seen her on the Tearnat's warship.

Pulling back, Torak looked down fiercely into River's eyes. "I am going to claim you, River. You have a choice. I can do it right here, right now. Or, I can take you back to my chambers in the North House and take you in a bed. What is your decision?"

"Here, now," River whispered.

Torak growled as he pulled back far enough to flip River over onto her stomach. Pulling the laces free on the back of her dress, he pulled her up onto her hands and knees so he could pull it down her shoulders. His breath caught as he realized she was not wearing anything beneath the dress.

"Kneel so I can pull the dress from you," Torak said harshly.

River pulled herself up until she was on her knees, her back still turned toward Torak.

"Stand," Torak growled, pulling River up until she was standing.

As she did the gown slid down her body to pool around her feet. She was left with only the knife strapped to her thigh and the one strapped to her forearm. Jo and Star had not brought her any underclothes explaining the women on this world didn't wear them. Star had been planning on making some to show the guys just how sexy underclothes could be.

Torak clenched his teeth. Seeing River standing nude with nothing but two knives attached to her was exhilarating. He was going to claim her as she wore them to honor her as the warrior she was. River started to turn around, but Torak gave her a stinging slap on her ass when she moved. River jumped at the slap. It hadn't really hurt her, just surprised her. She looked over her shoulder in surprise.

"You will not move unless I tell you to," Torak snarled, the mating heat taking over. He slowly began pulling off his clothes, walking around to stand in front of River as he did. He wanted to see her face as he stripped.

River's eyes widened, and she licked her suddenly dry lips as she watched Torak begin to remove his clothes. He removed his shirt first, slowly unlacing it. He watched as River's eyes followed his fingers as he undid each of the ties holding it closed.

When he paused, her eyes flew up to his before returning back to where his fingers were at. When he undid the tie she would lick her lips again. He did the same thing three more times, watching as her eyes would fly up to his before returning to his hands.

Torak was breathing heavily by the time he reached the buttons on his pants. River's eyes were glued to his fingers, which suddenly felt large and clumsy. He paused for a moment to take off his boots and socks, smiling when he heard River moan.

Straightening, his fingers returned to the buttons of his pants. He undid each one, watching as River's little pink tongue would dart out as he did it. He was so hard by the time he finished, he couldn't wait to get the suddenly heavy material away from his throbbing cock. Pushing his pants down, he kicked them aside, standing in front of River painfully aroused.

River's eyes were glued to Torak's fingers. Every time he would pause at a button she could feel her pussy clench in anticipation. She had almost gotten down on her knees and begged him to let her finish undressing him when he had stopped to remove his boots and socks.

She knew what he looked like naked. She had seen him in the shower. But nothing prepared her for what he would look like fully aroused standing before her. Unable to stop herself, she reached out her hand and gently ran the tips of her fingers over his swollen head.

"Beautiful," she breathed.

Torak jerked at the shy, gentle touch of River's fingertips across the head of his swollen penis. A deep growl rumbled in his chest as he dared her to do it again.

River looked up when she heard the deep growl rumble out of Torak's chest. Looking into his eyes, she saw a fire there that should have scared her, but it didn't. Instead, she felt more powerful, more beautiful, more desirable than ever. Sinking to her knees before him she had no idea what she was doing other than that she needed to taste him. Wrapping her hand around his thick cock, she pulled it toward her mouth, looking up at Torak for guidance.

Torak gazed down into River's beautiful face; her hand was wrapped tightly around his cock, and she was staring up at him as if asking his permission to taste him. The sweet innocence on her face caused his cock to jerk and throb.

"That's it, little one. Taste me," Torak whispered.

He pulled the pins from River's hair, letting it fall down her body. Grabbing a handful of it, he guided her mouth to his cock, groaning deeply as he watched it slide between her lips.

River could taste the warm musky pre-cum that was pearled on the tip of Torak's cock. It tasted so good she moaned as she ran her tongue over it. She loved the feel of Torak's hands wrapped tightly in her hair as he slid his cock deeper and deeper into her mouth.

She vaguely heard him tell her to relax so she could take more. What he didn't know was that she had practiced sword swallowing with the Amazing Kid Cozack, the world's best sword swallower. Kid had shown River how to overcome her gag reflex, and she had practiced sword swallowing for several years.

She still did it on occasion during some of their performances. Of course, they weren't real swords but compared to them, swallowing Torak's cock should be a piece of cake.

River pulled Torak's cock all the way out and licked her lips. Torak groaned in disappointment that River had not been able to take very much of his cock into her mouth. None of the females had been able to, as he was large.

He looked down at her, watching as her eyes smiled up at him. That was his only warning before she not only slid his cock into her mouth, but took the whole thing down to his balls. His eyes widened in disbelief. River wasn't done with him yet. Still watching his face, she began swallowing, letting the feel of the contractions of her throat massage his cock while she hummed.

The combination of the massaging of her throat and the vibration of the humming took Torak over the edge, and he shouted out his release, pumping his hot seed down River's throat. Only when she had drunk the last bit did Torak release his hold on her hair and slowly pull out of her mouth, shuddering as the long length moved over her tongue.

Collapsing to his knees in front of River, Torak stared at her in disbelief. He had never known of a woman capable of doing what she had just done.

River looked into Torak's eyes and smiled shyly. "Did you like that?" she asked softly.

Torak growled. "Like it? It was incredible. I am not sure I want to know where you learned how to do such a thing. I might have to kill the man who taught you." He felt jealousy raise its ugly head as he thought of the male who must have taught River how to give a man such exquisite pleasure.

River just smiled. She didn't really understand why he would be upset with The Kid for teaching her how to be a sword swallower. As far as she was concerned, Torak had his own sword tucked away in the front of his pants, and she was willing to swallow it any time he wanted her to.

"Now, little one, I believe it is your turn. You were very bad. I did not give you permission to give me release. I wanted you to feel pleasure before I did," Torak whispered huskily.

"But, I thought you liked it," River said, confused. She reached out her hand to touch Torak's face and hair. "You did like it, didn't you?" she asked softly.

"Oh yes. I liked it too well. It will take me a little while to recover so I can claim you. Until I am ready, I plan to pleasure you," Torak finished in a whisper.

River shivered at the promise. When Torak said he "planned to pleasure" her, it sounded more like he planned to "torture her with pleasure." If it was anything like she had experienced the other day, she could get addicted to being "pleasured."

Before River knew what was happening Torak had grabbed the leather tie from his hair and wrapped it around her wrists. Pulling them together he tied them together. He pushed her down until she was lying on her back on the blanket.

Sliding his hand down her body, he made a *tsk*ing sound when she arched up into his hand as he passed over her soft, curly mound. He moved his hand down to grasp the knife strapped to her thigh. Rolling over he pulled the knife out at the same time as he straddled her.

Grabbing her tied wrists with his one hand he plunged the long knife into a tree root above her head and tied the other end of the leather tie to it so her arms were stretched out over her head. River looked up to where her hands were tied and then back at Torak. He grinned down at her as he flicked both of her nipples with his fingers.

River let out a short yelp as the mixture of pleasure and pain swirled through her nipples as he flicked them again and again until they throbbed painfully. River wiggled under Torak trying to get away from the torture his fingers were doing to her nipples. Torak smiled as he watched River bite her lip over and over again as he flicked her nipples until they were swollen.

Oh, if only he had planned ahead, he could just see her with nipple clamps on those rosy pebbles. Next time, he would be prepared. Now, as he felt her bucking under him, moaning, he decided it was time to pleasure her some more.

Taking two of the long ties out of her dress he moved to each of River's ankles, looping a tie around each ankle before tying them off to two stakes in the ground near some plants. He would have to remember to tell the gardener to use more stakes in the future. They could come in very handy.

By the time he was done, River was tied with her hands above her head and her legs wide open. Noticing her nipples were not as swollen as before, Torak leaned down again and flicked them several times until River started sobbing again. Only then did he lean down and suck one of the swollen beauties into his mouth, watching River's face as he pulled, licked, and nipped it. When he was satisfied it was as swollen as it was going to get without clamps, he moved to the next one, giving it the same attention as he had the first one.

River screamed as Torak sucked her hard into his mouth. "Oh, Torak. Oh, Torak, please," she sobbed.

"What do you want, River? Do you want to feel me here?" Torak asked as he sucked on her swollen nipples. "Or do you want to feel me here?" He slid his finger into her pussy, pleased with how wet she was.

River arched her body, trying to take his finger even deeper. "Or"—his voice dropped even deeper—"do you want me to take you here?" He asked as he used her wet pussy juices to lubricate the tight ring of her ass before he slid a finger into it.

River jerked upward at his invasion into so private an area on her body. She bit back a moan, panting as he moved his finger around inside of her. "Know this, River, when I claim you, I claim all of you. There is no part of your body that will not belong to me. No part of your body I will not have loved, tasted, or taken. You will be mine. Totally."

River whimpered at the possessive tone in Torak's voice. She believed every word he said. She wanted him to take her every way he wanted.

"Torak, I need you," River whispered hoarsely. "Please, I need you."

"Not yet, love. You don't need me quite enough yet," Torak said as he pushed his finger into her all the way, loving the way her tight ass clenched around him.

* * *

River almost sobbed when she heard Torak's reply. She was on fire with need. She couldn't imagine him doing anything else to make her want him more.

Sobbing, she sucked in a shocked breath when she felt him spread her lips between her legs and cover her aching mound with his hot mouth. River had given up trying to breath; she had moved to panting as Torak sucked on her clit, pulling and tugging on it one minute, then licking and biting it the next. When he put one finger inside her pussy while another one continued to pump her ass, she didn't know what to expect. Her body began to shake as he continued to work her higher and higher, keeping her on the edge and not letting her come.

Torak wanted River so hot that when he claimed her for the first time she would never forget what it felt like to belong to him. He had long since been ready to come again, but this time was about River. He liked that she had never been fucked up the ass. He wanted to be the first and only one to have taken her there. He could feel her clenching on his finger as she came closer and closer to her orgasm.

Wanting to take it up another notch, he forced another finger into both her pussy and her ass. He knew he was larger, probably larger than any of the human males had been, and he did not want to hurt her when he claimed her. He felt River jerk, and her panting, increased as she felt the fullness of having two of his fingers in her ass at the same time as he was pumping her pussy. When she started to climax, he bit down on her mound, not moving his mouth or fingers until she sobbed her frustration.

Only when she finally wailed his name like she was going out of her mind did he pull himself up, gripping her thighs in both of his large hands.

Settling between her legs, he pulled her hips up until her pussy was level with his hard, throbbing cock.

"River, look at me," Torak demanded harshly. "Look at me as I claim you."

River was shaking her head back and forth, begging him to give her release. Torak watched as her small breasts swayed with the motion of her head. Torak let go of one of her thighs just long enough to give River a sharp slap to her overly sensitive mound, watching as she jerked her attention to him.

"Look at me, River, as I claim you," Torak repeated.

River kept her wide eyes on Torak's face as he repeated his claim on her. "You are mine. I, Torak Ja Kel Coradon of the House of Kassis, claim you, River, for my house and as my mate. I claim you as my woman. No other may claim you. I will kill any other that try. I give you my protection as is my right as leader of my House. I claim you as is my right by the House of Kassis."

As Torak finished repeating the traditional words he had spoken on-board the *Galaxy Quest*, he surged forward, pushing his thick, hard cock deep into River's womb with one strong thrust, never taking his eyes off her face as he claimed what was his. Torak felt the thin barrier break as he surged deeply into River. He knew with women in his world that meant she had never been with another man before.

A primal urge washed through him at the knowledge no other man had ever claimed River. She was his! Growling, Torak felt the roar rip from him at the same time River cried out. He couldn't have stopped even if he had wanted to. She was his.

Torak surged forward, burying himself all the way to River's womb in the one stroke. Holding her thighs in his hands, he watched as tears slid down from the corners of her eyes to drip onto the blanket below.

"I am sorry, River. I cannot hold back," Torak said. "You are mine, little one," he said hoarsely as he pulled back and surged forward again.

River knew once the initial pain of him breaking through her virginity passed there would be more pleasure than pain. She let the pain wash through her as her body adjusted to Torak's long, thick length. By the time he had pulled out almost all the way and pushed back into her for the third time, the pleasure had definitely returned tenfold. His grip on her thighs combined with her arms being tied had her hot. Moving her hips to match Torak's thrusts, River gasped as he hit nerve-ending after nerve-ending.

Torak growled as he pushed deep into River. He wanted more as he lost himself to the mating heat of his people. Pulling the knife out from the sheath on her forearm, Torak sliced through the leather tie holding River's wrists together. Without ever pulling out of her, he leaned back and sliced through the ties of her dress releasing her ankles. Only then did he withdraw all the way from River, grabbing her by the waist and turning her over onto her stomach.

"Get up on your hands and knees," Torak demanded, smacking River's ass when she didn't move fast enough.

River scrambled up onto her hands and knees as fast as she could with her body trembling with need. She still had not had an orgasm. Torak had built her desire to a fever pitch preparing her for his claiming.

Now, he was ready and so was she. River felt Torak a moment before he pushed into her as far as he could go from behind, grabbing her nipples between his fingers while he surged into her again and again. It was only when he pinched her swollen nub that she felt the release she had been seeking. It came so strong, so unexpected, she jerked as she screamed. Torak grunted as he felt his own release follow hers. He pushed his hips further, wanting her to take his seed all the way to her womb.

Torak grabbed River's hips when she jerked preventing her from pulling away from him as he continued to pump his seed into her from behind. The view of her long, dark hair tumbling around her while he watched his cock disappearing into her was a beautiful sight. He wanted her to come again and again. He had never seen such a beautiful sight as her coming.

Now, he waited as he let his body recover from his current release. During the claiming, the male needed to claim the female fully to complete the ritual so there was no way it could be disputed she was his. Already he could feel his body recovering as the mating heat flowed through him. The thought of taking her every way possible was a powerful aphrodisiac. He began pounding into her again, reaching around to play with her clit. When she whimpered and tried to pull away, he smacked her ass.

"You will come again. You are mine, and I will claim you again and again, River," Torak said harshly.

"Please," River moaned.

"I plan to please you, little one, over and over and over again," Torak said through gritted teeth. "Now spread those beautiful thighs for me so I can enjoy you as well."

River shuddered as she did as she was told. She spread her thighs even farther apart, groaning as it changed the angle of Torak's thrusts. She cried out when Torak returned to flicking her nipples until they were swollen. He grabbed them, rolling them as he moved fast, then slow in her pussy. When he changed his angle once again and brought her up and back until her back was pressed against his chest, she knew she was going to come again. Torak grabbed one of her distended nipples in one hand while his other rubbed her clit. He had spread his thighs, forcing her to spread even further. The force of having her legs spread while his cock was buried deep inside her was too much. River came again, fighting Torak as he held her in place.

River sobbed in Torak's arms. "Now, little one. Now, we can come together."

River shook her head. "I can't," she sobbed. "I can't take any more."

"Oh yes, you can. You can take this and much, much more," Torak whispered. "This is only the beginning."

River shuddered at the veiled promise. He was going to kill her with pleasure if this was only the beginning. She shuddered again as she felt him beginning to move again.

Torak smiled grimly as he bent River over. Now, they would come together. He was not sure if she was ready for him to claim her fully, but he would try. River had proven to be as spirited as he had hoped his mate would be. She was also a true warrior, fighting him as they made love as she fought him in all other areas. Now, she would match him.

"Can you take it, River? Can you handle what life would be like with me?" Torak challenged.

River growled at Torak. He wanted to know if she could take it. Well, he could just bring it on, she could take anything he had to dish out and more, she thought, suddenly feeling like she was the sexiest, most desirable woman in the galaxy. Pushing back against Torak, River suddenly knew she wanted to be claimed by him every way imaginable. She craved what he could give her just as she had craved the taste of him.

Torak could feel the change in River as she reached up to meet his challenge. Yes, she was his perfect mate. He loved how she felt when she began pushing back against him and rubbing her ass as if inviting him to try to take her. River glanced over her shoulder and suddenly jerked away from Torak pulling out of his arms and stood facing him.

Torak jumped to his feet, staring at her as she breathed in deeply. "If you want me, you have to catch me," River purred, moving away from him to run through the cover of the trees.

Torak jerked at the challenge to the primal part of his soul. With a wicked grin he took off after her. He knew she wouldn't go far, she wouldn't want to be seen.

Luckily, he had warned everyone to stay away from this section of the garden as he did not want to be disturbed during his wooing of River. Now, he was very happy he had insisted on their privacy, though he would have taken her in front of everyone if he had to. The mating claim would not be denied once started. Torak stopped, listening for a moment before a gentle breeze blew the scent of his mate to him. Moving out of the cover of the trees he waited a moment before he twirled around and raced back in.

River let out a surprised squeal as Torak suddenly returned to her hiding place. She had climbed the tree and waited silently, holding her breath, as he had come under the branch she had been standing on. When he had left, she had jumped down, planning on dashing back to the blanket where she was going to wait for him to return. Instead, he held her captive against a low-hanging branch.

"Mine," Torak growled, running his nose up and down River's jaw. He reached down with one hand, sliding his fingers into her wet pussy.

"Mine," he said again, bringing his fingers up and licking them.

River shivered with desire as she watched him. It was only when he pressed her into the branch, bending her over it and spreading her cheeks that she flushed, feeling her pussy clench and soak her thighs.

"Mine," Torak said, sliding his fingers through the juice running down her leg and rubbing it on the tight ring of her ass. "All mine," he said as he pushed his fingers into her ass stretching her.

River moaned at the burn of his fingers stretching her. She could feel her pussy reacting to his claim, knowing she could deny him nothing.

"Yours," she groaned spreading her legs even further in invitation.

Torak pushed River further over the branch until her ass was way up in the air. Pushing her thighs apart so it would spread her even further, he slid his cock into her wet pussy covering it with her natural lube while he continued stretching her ass with his fingers. He felt her clench around him as he pushed his cock slowly in and out of her. He watched as it disappeared. As he pumped her he ran his fingers through her juice wetting her tight hole and sliding first one, then two, then three fingers into it, stretching. River moaned as she pressed back against his fingers, feeling the fullness of having something in both her ass and her pussy at the same time.

"Now, River. I am making my final claim on you. Relax as I take you, little one," Torak said softly, pulling his hard cock out of her pussy and sliding it into the tight ring of her ass. He watched as it slowly disappeared into her, both of them panting as the burning of his thick cock broke through the tight ring of her ass and his feeling her fisting him like a glove. He continued pushing into her as he played with her clit, making her hotter and hotter.

"Oh yes, little one. Oh yes," Torak groaned as he sank all the way to his balls into her ass. He waited a moment to give her time to adjust before pulling it out partway. He pushed it back in slowly, each time pulling a little further out than before and pushing in a little harder.

River panted at the feeling of fullness. She was bent over the tree, spread wide-open for Torak. She wanted more, she needed more, she could feel the pressure from another orgasm building and needed to feel its release.

"Faster, oh, Torak, I need you to go faster," River moaned as she pushed back against him.

Torak slapped River's ass as he pushed in. "You want it hard and fast, little one, you'll get it hard and fast."

Torak gripped River's hips and began pounding her ass faster and faster going deeper until he couldn't go any further. He listened as she began a keening wail as her climax built to a breaking point. Torak knew he was not far from his own release. Pounding into River, he yelled out as he felt her squeezing him, the force of it sucking his own release out of him. Burying himself all the way, he yelled out his final claim on the alien warrior who had captured his heart.

Chapter 12

River smiled as she looked out over the city below, watching as a light rain fell. She had been in the North House for over a week now and couldn't believe the change. She had been introduced to all the residents who lived in the huge House.

It seemed the House was a much quieter, calmer place since all the females had been removed. There had been a fair amount of jealousy among the women, which had made life difficult for everyone, according to Jenta, wife of one of the security team members. River had met her one day while she was exploring the huge House.

Jenta and River had become friends. Jenta would often visit with River after Jo and Star had left for the day or in the evenings if Torak was busy. River had decided it would probably take her a year just to learn how to get around the North House. She had never seen so many rooms and passageways in her life. It made the underground catacombs of Paris look like a child's playground.

One thing she hadn't gotten used to was always having someone with her. Until the assassin was captured Torak would not let River go anywhere alone even in the house. Today, Kev Mul Kar and two of his other men were with her.

"Kev, do you know of a place where I can work out?" River asked as she turned from the window.

"There is a training room, my lady, on the lower level that might suit you," the Captain of the Guard replied softly. He had been watching her as she gazed out the window, privately enjoying how her figure was silhouetted against the huge window. River sighed. She really liked the Captain of the Guard, but it drove her nuts when the people here called her "my lady."

"Can you show me where it is? I haven't worked out in almost three weeks, and it is driving me crazy!" She asked turning to look at him.

Jo and Star wouldn't be coming over today. Star was working on the modifications for the dresses, and Jo was grounded for mouthing off to Manota again, which meant he wasn't letting her out of his sight.

"Of course, my lady," he replied with a bow.

River just rolled her eyes at Kev Mul Kar, watching as he fought to hide the smile curving his lips at her response to calling her by her title.

River stopped by her and Torak's rooms to change into something more appropriate for working out. She hoped Star was going to be finished with her new designs soon because the gowns were a pain in the ass. River pulled her black duffel bag out from under the bed and pulled out the black pants she had worn on the warship and a sports bra. She didn't have her shirt anymore as Torak had destroyed it when she had been shot.

Thankfully, Jo had rescued her other clothes. Pulling them on, she grabbed one of Torak's shirts and slipped it on over her outfit. It hung to her knees and covered her almost as well as the gowns did.

As she was closing the bag her eye caught on a shiny disk. River laughed as she pulled out not one, but almost a dozen DVD's.

She had forgotten all about them! She had found some old videos from when she, Jo, and Star had been little all the way through to two years ago when Jo and Star had left the circus. Walter, the ring master, had always been really big on videotaping everything and had made the disks for her. She would have to ask Torak, or Kev if they had a way of viewing them. Setting the disks aside on the table near the bed, she zipped the bag closed and slid it under the bed.

* * *

River looked around in amazement at the training room. It was like a huge indoor playground with ropes hanging from the ceiling, open areas covered in mats, climbing walls, hoops, loops, and every kind of obstacle ever imagined. River thought she had died and gone to circus heaven.

Kev Mul Kar swallowed past the lump in his throat as decided he had made a very serious error in showing Lady River to the training room. The lump grew when she kicked off the slippers she was wearing and dropped the shirt covering her. Standing with her back to him with her hands on her hips, he let his gaze travel over her figure.

Clad in black form fitting pants that showed off her sweet backside and long legs, he choked when he saw she was only wearing a small piece of material over her breasts. He heard the two other men groan when she suddenly pulled her leg straight up over her head standing on one foot while holding the other in her outstretched hands.

"Have you ever seen a body bend like that before?" The younger elite force member asked. "She isn't even moving!"

All three men gulped when River suddenly did a back bend, bending until she was actually looking out from in between her legs.

"I don't think a body is supposed to be able to do that, do you?" The other elite force member whispered.

For the next three hours the men panted, gulped, gasped, and sweated as they watched River twist, turn, bend, and flip in impossible positions. When she went over to where the targets for target practice were located they were left just shaking their heads in amazement as time after time she would hit the targets in the middle even after she had Kev blindfold her.

Torak came in just as Kev Mul Kar was untying the blindfold from River's eyes. He stood back in the shadows as he watched his Captain of the Guard. River said something to Mul Kar causing him to laugh. Whatever his response was, River must have liked it because she laughed in return smiling up at Mul Kar. Torak had enough when Mul Kar reached down and gently pushed a stray strand of River's hair back behind her ear.

"River," Torak called out as he strode over to where River and Mul Kar were standing. Torak's eye's narrowed as he took in the flush on River's cheeks and lack of clothing.

"Oh Torak, I had the most awesome time! This place is like having my own private playground!" River danced over to him.

Torak looked at Mul Kar with dark, cold eyes. "Why is she here?"

"Lady River wished to work out. This was the only acceptable place I could think of," Mul Kar answered calmly.

"What I have seen is not acceptable at all," Torak said with a deadly calm.

He was furious. No other male should be, seeing as much of River's body as she was showing right now. He let his gaze rake over River's scantily clad figure, before looking up at Mul Kar again.

One of the other men walked up holding River's knives. "Lady River, you are amazing. I have never seen a warrior do the things you have done today."

The other elite force member came up, laughing. "I have never seen a body be able to do the things she did."

Torak's gaze turned even colder as he watched River laugh at the two men. She took the knives from the one man, sheathing them around her body. When she bent over to slide four of them into the sheaths attached to her calves Torak had enough. The two younger men's eyes were glued to her rounded ass.

"Leave," Torak ordered, barely containing his anger.

The two younger men's eyes jerked up at the tone in Torak's voice. They quickly bowed, before heading for the door.

Mul Kar hesitated. "My lord, she is unaware of what she does," he said, looking over to where River had gone to get her shoes and shirt covering.

"Mind yourself, Mul Kar. She is mine. I will kill any man who thinks otherwise," Torak said coldly.

Mul Kar returned Torak's cold look for a moment before bowing his head and leaving.

River danced back over to Torak looking around for the other men. "Did they leave? I wanted to thank them for watching me today."

"That is not necessary. It is their job to protect you," Torak growled, reaching out to grip River's arm tightly.

"Hey, what's your problem? Did you have a bad day?" River had to practically run to keep up with Torak.

"Not until now," Torak said, his jaw hurting from clenching his teeth so hard. He was really trying to hold on to what little control he had.

"Oh. Well, what happened? Did someone run over your cat?" River asked breathlessly.

Torak stopped suddenly frowning. "What cat?"

River laughed at the confused expression on Torak's face. "It's just a saying. Things are only bad if you let them get to you," River said as she reached up and brushed her palm over Torak's face.

"River, we need to talk," Torak said softly, looking down into River's innocent blue eyes.

He ran his hand down her arm and pulled in a breath as he felt the silky, smooth skin of her stomach through the opened shirt. It reminded him of why he was so upset. He muttered a soft oath under his breath as he tried to get control of his anger and jealousy.

Turning, Torak pulled River through the passages until he came to their private living quarters. Pushing River inside, he turned and locked the door. Leaning back against it, he crossed his arms over his chest as he waited for River to look at him.

River felt a shiver run down her body. She knew Torak was upset though she didn't really know why. Moving toward the bedroom, she figured she'd give him time to cool off before trying to figure out what had him so bent out of shape. She walked over to the table and began pulling off the sheaths containing her knives, setting them down one at a time on the table near the window. She kept her back to the door even as she sensed Torak following her into the room.

"River, it is not acceptable for you to do the things you did today," Torak began firmly.

River froze before turning to stare at Torak as he began speaking. The more he spoke, the colder the look in her eyes became and the firmer her mouth compressed into a straight line.

"You are a member of this House, a female member. You will no longer be allowed to do the types of things you did today. Your place is to manage my household, greet my guests, and have my children, not flaunt your body before my men, teasing them and throwing knives. If you insist on such behavior I will have to take measures to punish you until you understand your place here. You will give me all your knives including your swords. In addition, I want the clothing you are now wearing and any other clothing resembling it. They will be destroyed so you won't be tempted to wear them again. I have had gowns made for you to wear and wear them you will. Do you understand?" Torak finished firmly, proud of himself for not losing his temper. He leaned back against the bedroom door satisfied he had shown River who was in charge.

River had listened to Torak at first in disbelief, then with growing anger. Her eyes were flashing blue flames by the time Torak was finished with his asinine demands.

"Let me see if I understand you correctly," River said slowly, picking up a knife from the table and tapping her chin.

"I am a female," she threw the knife. It hit right next to the left side of Torak's face, close enough that if he were to move a hairbreadth he would feel the cold blade. Torak froze, warily watching River.

She picked up another knife. "You think you can tell me what to do," she threw the knife, and it hit on the right side of his face exactly across from the one on the left. Torak felt a fine bead of sweat begin to form on his brow as he realized River was not finished.

Picking up another knife she ran her finger over the tip. "I am to manage this monstrosity," throwing the knife. It embedded in his left shirt sleeve, pinning his arm to the door.

Pulling four more knives out of the sheaths on the table, she threw them with such speed he didn't even see her hand move. "You think I am a tease, you can take my knives away from me, you can punish me, and I am to wear what you tell me I can wear," River growled coldly as each knife embedded itself in a different place around Torak's body, pinning him to the door.

Picking up one last knife Torak began to sweat openly at the look in River's eyes. "Oh, and let's not forget the most important thing. I am a bitch in heat who is supposed to spread her legs for you and pop out your children when you command it," River said as she threw the last knife. It landed snugly in the narrow space between Torak's slightly parted legs.

Grabbing the rest of her knives off the table, River pulled her black duffel bag out from under the bed and walked over to where Torak was pinned to the door. She looked him in the eye, daring him to say anything.

"Did I get it right?" She asked softly before stalking out of the room.

River was so mad she didn't even see Manota until she ran into him. She had swung open the door to the private living area having no idea where she was going to go, but knew she couldn't, wouldn't stay with someone who wanted to take away who she was.

"Oh, sorry," River muttered as she moved around Manota.

"Where is Torak? I need to speak with him," Manota called out after River. He was never going to understand these female warriors.

"In the bedroom," River called out, never turning around. "Go on in—he could probably use some help."

Chapter 13

"What happened to you?" Manota asked as he stood staring in disbelief at Torak.

"Just pull some of these damn knives out of my clothes so I can move," Torak gritted out.

Manota had walked through the living quarters after Torak had responded to his call for entrance. When he walked through the door of the bedroom he had stopped in concern when he saw Torak standing strangely still next to the door.

When he noticed his older brother couldn't move for all the knives surrounding him, he couldn't keep the bark of laughter from escaping. Pulling several knives out so Torak could move, he watched as Torak finished grabbing and pulling the rest of them out, grimacing as he pulled out the one between his legs.

"I take it River is upset with you," Manota said dryly.

Torak gave his brother a dirty look. "What makes you think that?"

"Could have been the knives holding you to the door or maybe the one between your legs. You have to admit, she is amazing when it comes to throwing them," Manota grinned.

"I'll make sure I ask her to give you a demonstration the next time I see her," Torak retorted.

Manota followed Torak into the next room. He watched as Torak pulled out a glass container filled with a dark amber liquid. Pulling the stopper, Torak poured a large glass of the amber liquid into it and downed the entire contents before refilling it. As he lifted the glass, he noticed his hand was trembling slightly. Gods, she had looked *so* beautiful when she was throwing those knives.

Looking down at the liquid swirling in his glass Torak asked absently, "Do you think all the warriors on her planet are like her, Jo, and Star?"

Manota gave a harsh laugh before replying. "Gods, I hope not. I wouldn't want to face them in a fight. If they didn't kill us first, they would wear us down with their beauty, their intelligence, their sense of humor, their loyalty, their…" Manota trailed off as he glanced out the window. Everything he was saying was what attracted him to Jo.

"I could use one of those," Manota said suddenly nodding toward the amber liquid. He poured himself a large glass, taking a healthy swig of it before moving to sit across from Torak.

Torak sat on the couch. "What did you come to see me about?"

Manota took another sip of the liquid before filling Torak in to what the security forces had found out so far about the assassination attempt. "It looks like Tai Tek is more than a little upset at your return. He had told the council of your capture and demise at the hands of the Tearnats. Imagine his disappointment when you reported in. The funny thing was he reported the death of the chancellor and you and your men before you had actually been captured. It seems he was a little too eager to for you to be dead to wait for the event to actually happen."

Torak sat back deep in thought. "You have proof of this?"

Manota smiled darkly. "Yes, our spies were very thorough. We have the actual vidcom of his announcement to the council."

Leaning forward, Torak put his hands on his knees. "What do you suggest we do?"

Torak watched as Manota stood up and refilled his drink. Manota was deadly when it came to espionage. He had spies everywhere and could kill as silently and efficiently as any assassin.

"I think a trap is fitting," Manota suggested. "He wants to take control of the House of Kassis. Twice now I have found plots against Father, though I couldn't prove he was directly behind them. Father has been gone to the Eastern region where Tai Tek knows better than to attack him. He will be back at the end of the week from the trade negotiations. I believe Tai Tek will try again," he added.

"No assassins can get into the House of Kassis now with the force field in place," Torak replied.

"No, but Tai Tek can. There will be a dinner celebrating the new trade agreement. As a member of the council, Tai Tek will be invited. Since it is in the South House it will be harder to secure than the other Houses. Tai Tek will have to be personally involved in the attempt. When he strikes, we will get him," Manota said with a smile.

"I do not like using Father as bait," Torak replied softly.

"Father was the one who suggested the dinner," Manota grinned.

"I should have known," Torak replied.

A knock at the door pulled Torak's attention away. Moving to answer it, he was surprised to see two of his elite force members standing at the door.

"What is it?" Torak demanded.

"It's Lady River, my lord. We need your assistance, if you please," one of the men mumbled.

"Is she hurt?" Torak asked, his heart dropping to his stomach as he brushed past the two men. "Where is she? Your team was supposed to be watching her at all times."

"She is well, my lord. We were trying to watch her, but she has not been cooperative," the other man said.

Torak and Manota followed the two security team members out of the North House and toward the East House. Halfway there the men stopped as they encountered a large number of the elite force standing near one of the garden structures. All the men stood still, looking up at the sky. Frowning, Torak and Manota looked up to see what had the men's attention. On a thin cable forty feet in the air was the small figure of his mate, just sitting there.

"How in the hell did she get up there?" Torak whispered, turning pale.

"What in the hell is she doing up there?" Manota asked.

As part of the garden decorations a series of eight pillars were placed between the North and East

Houses. The pillars were secured to each other by cables to prevent them from moving. There was a fifty-foot gap between each pillar. The pillars themselves were covered with a climbing vine that flowered during certain times of the year. River sat on one of the sections between the second and third pillar.

"There's another one!" One of the men shouted as they watched the small figure of Star move out onto the cable, followed by Jo.

"Oh gods," Manota groaned, watching as Jo tested the cable.

* * *

"Hey," Star said quietly, moving over the cable to sit next to River.

"Hey," River said glumly.

"Hey, guys," Jo said as she moved to sit next to Star. "What's up? Besides us."

River looked over at Jo and smiled. Jo always had a way of making a bad situation seem not so bad. River stared down at the growing number of people. She had watched as Torak had run down the path and knew she was probably in even deeper doo-doo than she was before.

"So... why are we sitting on a wire above everyone?" Star asked curiously.

River wiped a tear from her cheek. "Torak made me so mad! Then his security team wouldn't leave me alone."

"Oh," Star said, staring down watching as Jazin walked around in a circle pulling at his hair and rubbing his face with his hands. She had learned he seemed to do that a lot when she was around.

"So, what did he do that made you so mad you prefer sitting up here to being down there," Jo asked.

"He tried playing the 'I'm-the-man-do-as-I-say' card. He gave a long list of all the things I could and couldn't do." There was a moment of silence as the girls thought about what River had just said.

"So, what was on the 'could' list?" Star asked curiously, swinging her feet gently back and forth.

"Oh, I can wear dresses, greet his guests, have his kids, that kind of stuff," River replied sarcastically.

"Mm, and the 'couldn't' list?" Jo murmured, beginning to see the picture.

"I can't wear pants, work out, and I have to give up all my knives," River whispered as another tear slid down her cheek. "He even accused me of acting like a tease with his men. Why do guys have to be such jerks?"

All three girls sat on the wire looking down at the growing number of men gathering under them as word spread of the three female warriors sitting high in the sky.

Chapter 14

"What is going on?" A loud voice boomed over all the other voices. Silence fell over the crowd as a small group of men pushed their way toward Torak, Manota, and Jazin.

Ajaska Ja Kel Coradon, Leader of Kassis, strode through the crowd. He was a tall, imposing man like his sons. His long, black hair was pulled back at the nape of his neck, and he wore the traditional clothes of the warrior—black leather pants, dark shirt, and leather vest.

A faint scar ran across one cheek, a reminder of the battles he had fought in. He was still darkly handsome, looking not much older than Torak. Since the end of the war he had been leaving most of the day-to-day running of the Kassis government to Torak while he worked with other planets on developing trade agreements and dealing with the Alliance Council. As leader of the people living in the Kassis system, his duties had changed since the end of the war. Now, instead of leading warships in battle, he battled on the floor of the Council's Assembly.

Ajaska strode over to stand next to his three sons. He was shocked at their lack of acknowledgement. Never before had they failed to greet him upon his return.

"Torak, have you no greetings for me?" Ajaska asked, turning to follow his sons' line of sight. "What in the name of all the gods is that?"

"Not what. Who," Torak murmured distractedly. "Welcome home, father. As you can see we are a little busy right now."

"How are we going to get them down?" Jazin asked never taking his eyes off Star's small figure. His heart was in his throat as he watched her long legs swing back and forth like she didn't have a care in the world while on a thin cable forty feet in the air.

"I think we are going to have to wait until they are ready to come down. It will be too dangerous to try to forcibly remove them," Manota said, watching as Jo let go of the cable to stretch her arms high above her head. "Why doesn't she just cut my heart out with a dull knife? It would be a much less painful death," he muttered under his breath, sighing in relief when she put her hands back down.

"Who are they?" Ajaska asked intrigued.

"Ladies River, Jo, and Star. They are the female warriors from the Tearnat's warship, Your Grace. I gave you the report on them as soon as your sons filed it. Lord Torak has claimed Lady River as his mate," a nasal voice replied. "It is all in the report you read."

"What are they doing up there?" Ajaska asked, nodding as he remembered reading about female warriors. He had discounted it as an exaggeration.

"River is upset with me," Torak said, turning a little red.

Ajaska looked at his oldest son for a moment, realizing there was more to the report than he had been given. He looked back up at the three small figures sitting on the cable like some of the flying creatures in their world.

Turning, he looked at the man with the nasal voice. "Order everyone to leave. I will talk to the females."

Within minutes everyone was gone except Ajaska. He had even ordered Torak, Manota, and Jazin to return to their houses to wait for their females. They had protested adamantly before agreeing it might get the females down faster if they were not there.

Disgruntled, all three brothers left, swearing a long list of expletives under their breath as they did. Once Ajaska was satisfied everyone was gone, he walked under the wire to stare up at the three females.

"Come down," Ajaska ordered in a voice that had shaken even some of the strongest warriors in the galaxy.

He was used to giving orders and having them obeyed at once. He felt confident the three females would do his bidding and return to the safety of the ground. He confidently folded his huge arms across his chest and waited for them to obey him.

River, Jo, and Star looked down at the man standing under them. Jo stared at him with a wicked gleam in her eye before turning back to look at River and Star. None of them were in the mood to deal with any more arrogant men trying to tell them what to do.

"Ever heard the saying 'spit like a man'?" she asked right before she let a big glob of spit drop.

Ajaska jumped back as the glob landed near his foot. Soon he had backed up several feet, putting a safe distance between himself and the wire above.

River called down, grinning, "Would you like to rephrase that request?"

Ajaska looked at the three females and couldn't help but grin. They had fire!

Biting back a laugh, Ajaska called out. "Will you come down... please? I would like to meet the females who have caused my sons so much grief."

* * *

Torak heard a soft, feminine laugh followed by the deeper laugh of his father. He had been pacing the floor inside the front entrance for the past hour. When the door finally opened, it was to find his mate with her arm around his father's waist. His father was carrying River's black bag.

"Are you trying to kill me?" Torak asked frantically looking River over to make sure she was unhurt. He was going to beat her ass for scaring him so badly before he kissed her senseless.

River raised her eyebrow. "If I had wanted to do that you would have been dead a long time ago," she said coolly. She was still mad at him for being such a jerk earlier.

Turning to Ajaska, River leaned up and gave him a kiss on his cheek. "Thank you for listening. If you don't mind, I'd like to retire for the evening. I'll see you in the morning."

Ajaska ran the back of his hand gently down River's cheek before giving her a kiss on her forehead. "Good sleep, fierce warrior."

River just laughed shaking her head at his label of her. If they only knew, she thought, if they only knew.

* * *

Ajaska watched as River left the room, staring thoughtfully after her before turning to look at his oldest son.

"I could use a drink. I feel like the report I received was not nearly as detailed as it should have been," Ajaska said, walking toward the living quarters he used while in the city.

Torak was torn as he followed his father reluctantly. He wanted to follow River to their living quarters but knew she was still too angry with him to listen to anything he might have to say. With a resigned sigh, he turned to follow his father.

Ajaska handed Torak a glass filled with the dark amber liquid he had been drinking earlier and watched as his oldest son sat down on the edge of a chair.

"Tell me about her," Ajaska demanded softly.

For the next two hours, Torak talked about everything that had happened. He told his father how he had been stunned the first time he had seen River come out of the darkened corridor on the Tearnats' warship; how she had killed Progit and two other Tearnats before releasing him, Jazin, and his other men before sabotaging the warship; how she had killed Trolis when he had attacked Gril and himself in the shuttle bay; and her fight on his claiming of her. He left nothing out. His hands trembled as he recounted how she almost died while saving his life the day they had returned to the planet.

"She is the most beautiful creature I have ever seen," Torak whispered softly. "It is impossible to think of her as a warrior when I hold her in my arms. She is so soft, so delicate...so fragile. It takes every ounce of strength I have not to wrap her up and hide her away."

Ajaska sat quietly for a while before replying. "Torak, you have to let her be who she is. She is not like our women. If you had wanted one of our women you could have had your choice of them. Her spirit is as wild and beautiful as she is. If you try to take that away she will soon come to resent you, and the spirit you love so much will die. Is that what you want?"

Ajaska rose from his seat and walked over to a satchel he had hanging from a chair. Pulling a data screen from it, he handed it to Torak.

"Read this. It is from an old text found in the Eastern regions. I scanned it before I left after hearing about your warrior women." Ajaska said as he moved away.

Torak looked up at his father than down at the data screen. Touching it, he began reading slowly since it was in an old language of Kassis not known to many but their scientists who studied their ancient history. As a royal member of Kassis, he had learned the language as part of his training when he was younger.

"After the great wars, there will be those who oppose its end. Fear them, for they wear a false mask of loyalty. Beyond the edges of our galaxy will come three great warriors who will rise out of the shadows of hatred to free the sons of Kassis. These warriors carry the weapons given to them by the Gods: the blade of peace, the crossbow of honor, and the staff of justice. Only when the warriors and the sons unite as one can peace come to the House of Kassis."

Torak looked up at his father trying to comprehend what he was reading.

"What you have read is a thousand-year-old prophecy discovered almost three months ago carved into the stone of one of the temples in the ruins of Karazdin, the ancient city of knowledge," Ajaska said, quietly taking the data screen from Torak and replacing it in the satchel.

"You talked about the three female warriors' rescue of you, your brother, and your men. They appeared out of the shadows of a Tearnat's warship. A Tearnat filled with hatred who fought to continue the war and who wanted to kill anyone who supported the ending of it. What weapons did they carry?" Ajaska asked carefully.

Torak looked at his father, his eyes widening as he softly answered, "River carried two battle swords, Star carried a small crossbow, and Jo carried a double-bladed staff," he whispered.

"Perhaps you should not be so willing to wrap your mate up just yet," Ajaska replied, looking down to stare at the amber liquid in his cup.

Chapter 15

Torak spent another hour with his father discussing the plan to trap Tai Tek should he make a move at the dinner to assassinate members of the House of Kassis. After making plans, Torak bid his father good sleep and retired to his and River's private quarters.

Opening the door to the bedroom, Torak walked over to the bed and gazed down at River's sleeping form. He loved her so much it shook him to the core of his being. When he was not with her, he was always thinking of her, worrying about her, fearful of another attack that might prove successful. Twice now he had felt the overwhelming fear of losing her. He never wanted to feel that fear again.

Torak quietly pulled his clothes off and slid into bed next to River, gathering her small form against his. Burying his face in her hair, he breathed in deeply.

"Torak?" River asked sleepily.

"Yes, little one," Torak replied, gently stroking her back.

"I'm sorry I threw the knives at you," she said, snuggling closer to his warm, hard body.

"I'm sorry I said the things I did. I shouldn't want to change you. I love you just the way you are, little one. I love you very much," Torak whispered into her hair.

River slid her leg up, brushing Torak's crotch. "I love you, too," she said, turning her face and kissing his shoulder.

Torak felt himself respond to her sensuous movements. River rubbed her body against Torak's, sliding her leg between his, running her hands down until she could stroke his growing length, placing tiny kisses over his shoulders and chest.

Torak groaned as he felt her slide down his body. Rolling on top of him, she ran little kisses and nips down his stomach before taking his cock into her mouth. Torak spread his legs further apart, becoming more aroused as River's long hair caressed the skin on the inside of his thighs. River lifted just enough to slide his long, thick length deep into her throat swallowing it. Torak gripped the sheets in both hands to keep himself from jerking.

"Oh gods," he moaned loudly, fighting to keep from bucking against her as she pulled out and then swallowed his cock again and again.

"Oh gods!" Torak yelled loudly, arching up into River as he felt his release burst from him. He was shaking so bad from the overwhelming feelings, he thought he was going to lose his mind as River used her throat to massage his cock until she had swallowed every bit of his hot seed.

"I don't know how you do that," Torak panted, groaning as River pulled back to sit between his legs, smiling shyly at him. Gazing up at her, Torak couldn't believe how lucky he was to have her.

"You are amazing," Torak said with a grin. "Now, it is my turn."

River laughed as she pulled her nightgown over her head. Torak licked his lips as he watched her beautiful breasts pull free of the coverings. Sitting up, he cupped her breasts in his hands, running his thumbs over the swollen nipples.

"River, I want to love you tonight like I have never loved you before. Will you trust me?" Torak asked. "I promise it is only your pleasure that I seek," he murmured as he drew one of her nipples into his mouth.

River felt a shiver of excitement run through her at the promise of sweet pleasure. Leaning forward, she pulled his face up to meet hers, kissing him softly on the lips. "I trust you with my life. Take me, Torak. Take me to new heights."

Torak smiled, nodding. "You will do what I say from this moment on."

He smiled when River raised her eyebrow. "Only in the bedroom, little one. I will only request you do what I tell you while in the bedroom. We will work on it outside of it."

River smiled her agreement before letting out a squeal of laughter as Torak grabbed her around the waist, pulling her up to stand on the bed. "Stand there. Do not move."

River nodded silently as she watched Torak move to a set of drawers and opened them. He pulled out several items laying them out carefully on the bed before turning to River.

"You are mine, River, after tonight you will never forget that. I promise you," Torak said as he gently wrapped straps around each of River's wrists.

Shivering as desire flooded her body, River watched as Torak attached each strap to a bolt in the ceiling above the bed, stretching her arms over her head until she was standing on her tiptoes. The straps were positioned just far enough that it spread her upper body, forcing her breasts up. Moaning, River could feel the moisture between her legs at the thought of what was to come.

Torak smiled as he noticed River's reaction. "Anticipation can be a very powerful aphrodisiac, River. I want to keep your body on edge so when I finally let you come you will feel it throughout your entire body."

Kneeling on the bed, he picked up a blindfold. "You are used to this, aren't you, River? You like to be blindfolded," he whispered, tying it over her eyes.

"The blindfold will help you visualize what I am doing to you. Only when you are ready will I let you see exactly what I am doing," Torak said softly.

River turned her head as she followed the sound of Torak's voice. She was beginning to pant, wondering what he had in store for her. Her imagination was taking off as she remembered how he had taken her in the garden. They had made love many times since that day, but never like they had that day.

River gasped as Torak touched her nipple with something cold and hard. Trying to pull away from it, she found she couldn't move very far hanging the way she was. She jerked in surprise as he sucked deeply on her nipple, pulling the nipple into a hard peak. When he released it, she thought he was going to suck the other nipple the same way. Instead, she felt a pinch, then a wave of pleasure, and pain flooded her as he attached the first clamp on her.

"Oh God," River groaned, feeling him move to her other nipple. Now that she knew what was happening the knowledge the other nipple was going to feel the same pleasure/pain had her panting.

"Anticipation, River," Torak said as he sucked her nipple into a hard peak.

River screamed out as he attached the other clamp. "Beautiful," Torak said as he brushed both her nipples.

River let her head drop forward as she listened to Torak move again. She was awash in a heat so hot she felt like she was going to burst into flames at any moment. Her head jerked up when she heard the sound of a chain.

When Torak grabbed her first nipple and pulled the chain through the clamps making sure it caressed her sensitive nub, she groaned loudly. Torak smiled as he slid the chain through the nipple clamps and attached them so he could pull on them when he was ready. Now, he needed to get the rest of her body ready for him.

Walking around River, Torak ran his hands down her back, letting his large, callused hands rub her sensitive skin. "You have such a beautiful ass," Torak said as he spread her cheeks. "Soon, little one, soon you will watch me as I take you there," Torak said as he gently took a large butt plug he had lubed and pressed it against her tight ring.

He pushed slowly, letting her body adjust to it as he pushed it into her. He watched as the bulbous head disappeared inside her. He closed his eyes as he felt a hot shot of desire flow through his body as he remembered how sweet it had been under the trees with River bent over as he claimed her. He wanted her again desperately.

River cried out as the combination of the clamps on her nipples and the burning of the butt plug triggered a response. "Please!" River let her head fall forward again as she breathed deeply.

"I promise to please you, River," Torak said as he moved, sinking to his knees in front of her.

Pulling her legs apart, he draped one leg over each of his shoulders, pulling her wet mound toward him. River was sure he was going to give her relief; instead she felt something hot slide over it. Crying out, she jerked. Torak was using one of the laser hair removers on her to remove all the curls covering her. She recognized the feel from when Jo had shown her how to use one the first time to shave her legs and underarms. Jo had bragged that she would never have to shave again.

"You are too beautiful to be hidden, River. When I look at you, taste you, I want to see it uncovered," Torak said softly, running the laser over and over her until all that was left was soft, smooth skin.

Torak ran his fingers over the silky mound, cooing at River when she jerked and cried out. Torak buried his fingers inside River, feeling to see how wet she was. Almost, he thought, reaching under her to twist the butt plug. River arched, and Torak opened his mouth to pull her swollen clit into his mouth. Yes, it was definitely more beautiful uncovered. Spreading River's lips, Torak ran his tongue over her, lapping at her until she was sobbing.

Torak reluctantly pulled River's legs off his shoulders until she stood on her tiptoes again. She was beautiful hanging there, and he wanted her to see just how beautiful she was as he made love to her. Pulling the blindfold off, he gave a command, and all the walls in the room shimmered, turning into a mirrored surface.

River stared in disbelief at her reflection. She looked like a wild creature. Her hair was flowing down around her in waves. Her arms were stretched high above her head showing off her willowy figure.

A chain hung from the clamps attached to her nipples, and the most feminine part of her was bare. She had small love bites on the insides of her thighs and on her breasts, but it was her eyes that she was the most shocked over. Her dark, dark blue eyes shone with a wild flame of desire as she took in the reflection of her naked body hung as an offering for Torak.

Torak's naked form stood next to River running his hands over her body in a sensuous path, pulling on the chain between her nipples and sliding down to cup her bare mound, spreading her lips so she could watch as he played with her clit.

River's eyes were glued to Torak's hands as he slowly pulled her feminine lips apart so he could slide his fingers over it. "Look how beautiful you are. Watch as I claim you, River. Feel me as I take you."

River couldn't have pulled her eyes away from what he was doing even if she wanted to. Torak undid the clamps on her breasts, smiling as River gasped while the blood flowed back into them. He released River's arms from the straps, pulling her down onto the bed where he slowly laid her back, spreading her legs so he could lie between them.

"Look up at the ceiling, do as I say, and watch as I take you," Torak murmured his voice thick with desire. "Play with your nipples. I want to see you play with them while you watch me taste your sweet pussy."

River moved her hands up to her breasts and began playing with the tips, groaning at how sensitive they were. Her eyes widened as she focused on what Torak was doing. He was playing with her clit, rolling it back and forth between his fingers while he used his other hand to gently twist the plug nuzzled in her tight ring.

Moving his fingers so they slid deeper into her vagina while he gave sharp twists to the plug gave the impression of her being fucked in both places at the same time. When he leaned down to drink her sweet juices, River shattered. She felt the flow of her juices soaking Torak's face. He moaned and drank deeply until she arched up, crying out for mercy as one orgasm flowed into another.

"Not yet, love. There will be no mercy tonight. I have only just begun," Torak said as he gently stroked River, watching her eyes widen as he tied her ankles to the end of the bed and moved to retie her wrists.

"All night," he promised as he slid his thick, heavy cock into her swollen pussy.

Torak finally let River fall into an exhausted sleep as the sun began rising over the mountains. He untied the cords holding her down. He had taken her over and over, bringing her higher and higher each time until she totally shattered.

The last time he had taken her, she had been tied face down to the bed. He had made sure she could turn her head and watch as he had taken her from behind. He had taken her until she screamed out her release, thrashing as she fought the restraints, her body quivering and shaking as she squeezed him.

He had felt the same release time and time again, coming as she fisted him tightly in her body, milking him until he was on the verge of collapse himself. He loved how wild and trusting she was, letting him do whatever he wanted to her body. Never had he felt so satisfied. He lay holding her in the safety of his arms until the sun peaked over the mountains shining down on the city below.

There was much to do before the trap to catch Tai Tek was set, but even so, he was reluctant to leave the comfort of River's body sheltered next to his. Torak ran his hand down her back and over the curve of her ass. He thought of the prophecy his father had him read last night. Was it possible River and her sisters were the warriors it spoke of? How could such small, delicate, beautiful creatures be such strong warriors? Would she be happy here, so far away from her world? He knew he could never survive her leaving. He would never let her go, even if she were to ask it of him. He couldn't do it before, and he knew he wouldn't do it now.

River turned over, snuggling closer to Torak. Torak smiled at her unconscious seeking of him. He ran his hand down her again, gently cupping one breast before moving over her stomach. Suddenly his hand trembled, and he laid it over her flat belly.

What if she was breeding? It was possible. He had not used anything to prevent it from happening. The idea of River round with his child caused a sharp pain of desire to flood his body. He wanted to see her swollen with his child. He wanted to see his child suckling her breasts. Torak smiled as he let his hand rest for a moment more on her. He knew deep down, she would never leave him if she was with child. A determined smile curved his lips.

Yes, there is much to do, he thought.

Chapter 16

Torak slipped quietly from the bed and showered. He was supposed to meet with his father and brothers in the planning room. He walked over to the bed one last time to gaze down at River. A soft chuckle escaped as he heard her soft snore.

She was exhausted. Leaning over he brushed a kiss across her forehead before straightening up. As he did his elbow knocked some disks lying on the small table next to the bed onto the floor. Torak bent to pick them up, frowning as he did so.

Where had these come from? He wondered.

Turning one of them over, he saw an image etched into the silver metal. Turning it so the light filtering through the windows shone on it, he gasped as a picture of a very young River, Jo, and Star appeared. Staring at it in amazement, he looked at the others.

Each one had pictures of the three girls though at different times of their lives. Looking at River sleeping so peacefully, Torak grinned. He wanted to know what was on the disk. If it gave him some clue about River's world before him, he wanted to know. Stacking the disks up, he gave the command for the window to darken and quietly left the room.

* * *

Jazin looked up as Torak came into the planning room.

"I thought I was going to have to send the elite force to find you this morning, brother. It is unlike you to be late to a meeting," Jazin teased, seeing the relaxed way his brother walked.

Torak just grinned. "If the night had lasted any longer I would not have had the strength to attend."

Jazin looked at Torak with envy. "I wish I could say the same," he muttered.

Manota looked at Jazin with wide eyes. "You also?" he said in surprise. He thought he was the only one unable to tame a female warrior.

Jazin blushed as his father looked up and stared at him, then at Manota. "Tell me."

Jazin and Manota both turned a bright red. Only their father would demand they tell such a thing. How were they to admit they had not yet claimed the other two female warriors? Oh, they had tried, but the females were being most uncooperative about it.

Torak laughed loudly. "Oh yes, please do tell," He was feeling very good right now. Not only had he claimed his female warrior, but he was going to make sure she had no way of escaping him.

Manota looked at Torak in disgust. "You do not have to be enjoying our discomfort so much," he retorted.

"Oh yes, I do. How many times have I had to live with you and Jazin making my life hell?" Torak responded, sitting back to watch his brothers squirm.

"Torak, you are not helping matters. Must I remind you of what the prophecy states? *'Only when the warriors and the sons unite as one can peace come to the House of Kassis.'* Let them explain," Ajaska said sternly. He sat down at the long table and folded his hands, waiting.

"What prophecy?" Jazin asked.

"Later. Tell me why you have not claimed the female warriors," Ajaska said, looking sharply at his two younger sons. He would not let them distract him.

Manota ran his hand over the back of his neck. "Jo is the most hardheaded, stubborn, frustrating female I have ever met! I should just spank her ass, tie her down, and claim her, but I am afraid she would probably slit my throat when she got loose just to prove she could," Manota said, feeling overwhelmingly frustrated. He didn't know what to do.

"Is she not attracted to you?" Ajaska in surprise.

"No, she is attracted to me all right. Her kisses are…" Manota's voice faded as he looked down at his hands. "She has family back in her world… her parents. She is not sure she can commit to me because she feels she must return to them."

"Star is the same. She cannot commit to me knowing her sister may leave and at the idea of causing her parents so much pain at not knowing what has happened to her and Jo," Jazin said softly. "It is causing her great distress."

Puzzled, Ajaska turned to Torak. "Why does your mate not have these same feelings?" He wondered.

Torak looked at his father and brothers. "I don't know."

"Perhaps there are answers in these. I found them next to our bed. They have images of River, Jo, and Star on them. Jazin, can you see if you can download the data from them?" Torak said, pushing the pile of disks at Jazin.

Jazin reached for them, turning them over and over. He nodded. "It shouldn't be too difficult. I can scan them while we work and see if I can decipher the information."

Jazin pulled a scanner out from his waist and slowly ran it over each disk, pulling the information into it. Next, he asked the computer to decipher the information and to let them know when it was completed. Perhaps the information on the disks would help him and Manota understand why Jo and Star were so reluctant to accept their claim on them.

Nodding to the other men, they began discussing their strategy for capturing the man or men behind the assassination attempt on Ajaska and Torak.

"The dinner is planned. Kev will be in charge of security for the South House. He is working with Manota's and Jazin's Captains of the Guards. Each will have men acting as servers during the dinner. In addition, he has set up additional screens in the force field that will allow us to track each person entering the House. A link will be sent to each of us showing where a person is at any given moment," Torak began.

"How can he do this?" Ajaska asked, surprised. The force field was good at keeping out anyone who had not been given permission to enter, but once they entered their security, they had never been able to track specific individuals before.

"Thanks to Manota, it can now be done. He has been working on it for the past year and has created a digital mapping of each person's genetic marker. Even if they were to use a disguise, it will tell who they really are." Torak said.

"Does anyone else know of this?" Ajaska asked curiously.

"No," Manota said. "I don't want to share it as yet until we catch the man or men behind the attempts on you. It will become useful once the Council assembles again, though."

Nodding his head, Ajaska turned back to Torak. "Continue."

"Jazin will cover the gardens. He will monitor anyone who comes and goes through the garden areas as the force fields will be focusing on protecting the other three Houses. The gardens will be accessible to the guests as is customary during formal dinners. Manota will be covering the South House. He will monitor anyone who is in any of the levels, including the lower levels and roof where the assassin tried before," Torak's eyes grew dark as he remembered the day he almost lost River.

"Father and Torak will be at the front entrance greeting everyone. Torak will attach a small vidcom to Tai Tek as he enters as well as attaching one to any of his guests or known allies," Jazin added picking up a vidcom so small it was almost impossible to see on the tip of his finger. "Another of Manota's inventions."

Ajaska looked amused as he studied it. "Remind me never to make you mad," he teased his middle son.

"Once everyone has arrived, we don't think Tai Tek will try anything too soon. He has to give the impression of being the loyal councilman, he was elected to be. After dinner when people are mingling is when we think he will try to strike. He will of course try to maintain a high profile so he has plenty of witnesses to vouch for him. Father and Torak will be the main targets and will be acting as the bait. If he or any of his guests try to draw either of you away, go with them. We will be watching both of you at all times. We will also be looking at anyone who is not who they appear to be. If you have a doubt, just touch your left eye and an image of the person will appear. Manota will show you how to use the eye lens before the dinner. They are good for about four hours before they dissolve. Once Tai Tek makes his move we will surround him and take him out," Torak finished. "Are there any questions?"

The men talked for almost another hour going over different possible scenarios and fine-tuning their plans. They were just finishing when the computer chimed to let Jazin know the deciphering of the disks was completed. He glanced down at the data and was surprised to see it was a type of video.

"We might be more comfortable in the common room watching it," Jazin said. "I don't know about you, but I didn't eat this morning and could use some refreshments."

As the men were walking out of the planning room they heard the sound of soft, feminine laughter coming from the common living area they used when they had company. Torak walked into the room and stared at the three females sitting around drinking a hot liquid they called "coffee." River had made Torak figure out how to replicate the beverage shortly after she had moved into the North House.

Torak smiled softly as he watched River lean over and brush a stray curl away from Star's cheek. The love the three females had for each other was obvious. He felt fortunate River had not fought his claim as long as her sisters were doing. He didn't know if he would have had the self-control not to take her, by force if necessary.

"Something smells good," Torak said as he went over to give River a kiss.

River blushed. He had said that same thing to her during the night while he was licking her.

"Behave," she whispered softly, kissing him back.

"Never," Torak replied as he nibbled on her neck.

Manota and Jazin cleared their throats loudly. "We're hungry," they both said at the same time looking at Jo and Star with a deep hunger in their eyes.

The two sisters blushed and burst out laughing. "We are not on the menu this morning. There is plenty of other wonderful stuff, though. I don't know what everything is. The cooks in these Houses of yours are awesome," Jo said, waving a hand toward the table.

"River, I found some disks in the bedroom. Jazin was able to decipher them. Would it be permissible to you if we were to watch them?" Torak asked gently. He did not want River to think he was trying to go behind her back or upset her.

"You did! Oh Torak, I love you!" River said as she threw her arms around his neck giving him a big kiss.

"Jo, Star, I had forgotten all about them. Walter made me some home movies of the three of us from when we first met until you guys left two years ago. I was going to surprise you with a copy of them, but didn't have a chance to make them. I found them again the other day in my bag and was going to ask Kev or Torak if they could somehow convert them. Thanks, Jazin, for doing it," River said, ignoring the way Torak growled when she said his Captain of the Guards' first name.

"What is on them?" Manota asked, sitting down next to Jo with a plate overflowing with food.

"Just wait, you'll see!" River replied with a mischievous grin.

She settled back against Torak's legs on the floor. All the men sat back with plates piled high with food. Star let out a groan when Jazin pulled her between his legs. Jo just gave Manota a look that said "don't even try it" before sitting between him and Ajaska. Jazin gave the computer the command to start the vidcom it had uploaded from the disks.

"Oh. My. God." Jo groaned as she buried her face into Manota's shoulder. "I didn't think you meant from the *very* first time."

On the screen appeared three very young girls. River was five, Star was seven, and Jo was eight. They were all dressed in ballerina costumes and were chasing each other around on a huge net several feet off the ground.

"Hey, Walter," yelled five-year-old River. "This is Jo and Star. They are going to be my new sisters!" River giggled as Jo started tickling her. Star was prancing around, waving at the camera.

"Oh. My. God," River said as tears spilled down her cheeks. "There are my parents with yours," she whispered to Star and Jo, leaning forward. "Look how young they were."

The four men had forgotten all about eating as they watched the vidcom. Walter, whom Torak had heard River talk about several times, was a male, approximately three feet tall if he was an inch, who wore a red costume and a hat half as tall as he was.

As the videos continued he saw a young River slowly growing up. The video had plenty of shots of her, Jo, and Star together, but also of each one with different people, unusual people. When the video showed a man named Kid Cozack, a man of about thirty to River's eight, teaching her how to swallow a sword, he cringed at first; then his eyes grew wide with sudden understanding. If she could swallow a sword, then she wouldn't have any problems swallowing... He gulped.

"So that's how you know how to do that," he murmured in disbelief.

"Know how to do what?" Manota asked, glancing over to Torak who had an expression of awe on his face before looking at River's face which was a bright, bright red.

Torak looked at Jo. "Do you know how to do that?" he asked with a grin.

"Of course, Kid taught all three of us how to do it. Why?" Jo asked, puzzled, looking at Torak.

It wasn't until she looked at River's face that she understood what else could be swallowed. Jo turned as bright a red as River and shot Torak a look that spoke of severe pain should he say anything else on the subject.

Torak grinned really big before replying, "I only hope you find out one day, brother. Both of you. It is a most incredible thing."

Manota and Jazin looked at each other, puzzled, before shrugging their shoulders. River, Star, and Jo looked like they would like to do nothing better than crawl under the couch. River might have attempted to escape if Torak hadn't put his food down and pulled her onto his lap. She suspected it was to cover the very large bulge that was protruding from it.

All of them watched the vidcom for the next two hours, pausing it at times when the men needed clarification about some of the things they had seen. When Marcus the Magnificent cut River in two for hiding all of his rabbits, Torak had been overflowing with questions as to if it hurt, why would a man do such a thing, how could she have survived it, and what did she mean, he did it more than once. Jazin and Manota both had to be told numerous times to loosen their holds on Jo and Star when they watched them flying through the air, walking on the tight ropes, or falling through fire. None of them could understand the clowns were just men and women in makeup doing outrageous things.

The more they watched, the more confused, they became. They saw magnificent buildings and a world that was in some ways similar to theirs but vastly different in others. The technology they saw was primitive compared to theirs. They saw women working right alongside the men, many doing things females on their planet would never be allowed to do.

When all three of the men saw some of the costumes—or rather lack of costumes—the girls wore in front of so many other males, the room filled with growls except for the chuckle coming from Ajaska. Walter was their biggest mystery. He bossed and ordered everyone around no matter that he was a fraction of their size.

When Walter showed the performance dedicated to River's parents, she broke down in tears, burying her face in Torak's chest. He wrapped his arms around her tightly, trying to calm her as she cried.

"River's parents were killed in a fire at the hotel we were supposed to be staying at. There had been a mix-up with the arrangements. Almost all of us were at another hotel a block away. River's parents wanted to stay at the one originally booked because it was where they had met. River stayed with us to give her folks some privacy. They never had a chance. The stairwell exit had been chained closed against fire regulations. They died of smoke inhalation," Jo said softly, coming over to rub her hands on River's back while Star rubbed her hair. "It took River almost a year to recover. She heard the sirens and had raced down the street. When she couldn't find her parents, she rushed into the building. When the firemen pulled her out she was barely alive."

Star continued. "River was only seventeen at the time. She came to live with me, Jo, and our parents, but the circus was her family, too."

River looked up, her lips trembled as she stared at Star. Softly she whispered. "They wrapped me in their love. They loved my parents so much. I can still hear Walter announcing them, 'The Magnificent God and Goddess of the Blade, Godwin and Godiva Knight, and their daughter, River.' No one could throw a knife like my dad."

Star leaned over and gave River a hug before moving back to sit next to Jazin. "We had more moms, dads, aunts, uncles, and grandparents than any girl should ever have. Forget about getting a date! If a boy ever had the nerve to even ask they had to go through every person there."

"Yeah, remember the one that finally made it as far as Walter?" River laughed, looking at Jo.

"Jo had this one boy who wouldn't leave her alone. He was to the point he was almost stalking her as we went from town to town. Anyway, he decided to sneak into where we were staying one night. He made it as far as Jo's room before Walter surprised him," River continued laughing.

"Yeah, surprised him so bad he peed his pants when he pulled the covers down to give me a kiss and found Walter's ugly mug there instead," Jo laughed.

Manota growled. "Walter killed this male?"

Jo looked at Manota in disbelief. "Of course not. He sat the poor kid down and told him if he ever came back he was going to put him to work mucking out the elephant pens."

Star chuckled. "Yeah, now he has two performances a day with the damn things."

"Perhaps I am missing something. I have seen many of your people, some doing incredible things, but I have not seen you battle anyone. How is it this Walter did not capture your battles with your enemies?" Torak asked, puzzled.

River, Jo, and Star looked at each other before bursting out laughing. "We aren't warriors. We are as far from being warriors as you guys are from being... Well, let's just say a long, long way from being warriors. We are performers. We make people laugh and forget their troubles for a little while. People come from all over to watch us perform death-defying acts just for fun. We've never had to fight anything worse than maybe a bad cold before all this happened," River explained.

All four men just stared at the three females in stunned silence.

Chapter 17

"They are not warriors!" Torak growled again at his father.

All the men had been stunned as the women told them they were just performers for a thing called a circus. It was what they did to support themselves. They explained they did not have a male to take care of them and that it was not an uncommon thing in their world.

Women often lived and worked all alone without males in their lives. Their world did have warriors, even female ones, but they fought using different weapons and one had to go into the military which none of them had ever done. When River explained how she had come aboard the Tearnat's warship, how she had hidden in the hopes of finding a way to release her friends, and how they had taken turns learning more about the ship and stashing items they thought they might be able to use to escape using only the skills they had learned from the circus, Torak, Manota, and Jazin had all been horrified.

"The prophecy says three warriors will come carrying the items your women carried. I tell you they are the warriors the prophecy talked about!" Ajaska insisted.

"Father, they had never killed anything in their lives until they boarded the Tearnat's warship," Jazin began.

It explained so much to him now. How gentle and sensitive Star was. Why she had looked so scared the first time he saw her. Why she often cried out during the night.

"In the name of all the gods and goddesses, they did not even know life exists outside their galaxy! The furthest their people had gone was to their moon, and it wasn't even that far!" Manota exploded. "Now you expect them to fight alongside us knowing that we know this?"

"Yes. I do," Ajaska replied softly. He watched as all three of his sons looked at him in stunned silence, wondering if he had lost his mind. "They are the three warriors. I am sure of this. Look what they have done so far. Do not underestimate their skills. Just because they have not been trained as warriors does not mean they are not warriors."

"I have almost lost River twice. I will not take the chance of losing her again," Torak said harshly, turning to look out the window. "I will send her to our country estate until the threat is resolved."

"No," came a soft reply from the door.

Torak spun around. Standing in the doorway were River, Jo, and Star. Each of the women stood perfectly still. River glided into the room. She was wearing a pair of pants that looked almost like the long part of a gown. Around her waist was a jeweled belt. Her top had a sequined, scooped neck with billowing sleeves caught tight at her wrists. She had her hair braided so it fell in a long rope down her back. She looked so beautiful, so fragile, so… mad.

Torak groaned. The last time she had had a look in her eye like that he had ended up pinned to the door of their bedroom. He shifted his gaze to make sure he was standing far enough away from anything she could use should she begin throwing her knives again.

"River," Torak began softly.

"Don't you 'River' me. I am not going to be sent anywhere. Your father is right. We may not have been trained as warriors, but we know how to fight and to defend ourselves and those we love," River said, coming to stand in front of Torak. She placed her palm on his chest over his heart. "You said you would not change who I was. Now accept who I am."

Jo and Star stood just inside the door. "That goes for us too," Jo said softly. Star nodded her agreement.

River moved to sit on the low couch. "If Tai Tek is behind the assassination attempts, then I have a vested interest in capturing him." She gently touched her chest and the small, barely visible scar. "I owe him a return favor."

Torak's eyes darkened at the reminder. He crossed the room to kneel in front of River. "River, it will be too dangerous. I will not allow you to be in harm's way. Please, little one, I could not live if something should happen to you," he pleaded softly, holding her hands in his.

River leaned forward and brushed her lips against his, softly replying, "Then keep me safe by letting me help you."

"Besides, wouldn't it look a little funny if suddenly all three of us were to disappear? I mean, River is your wife...uh, I mean, mate. If you show up at this dinner without her, isn't that going to make the bad guys suspicious?" Jo asked, looking at Manota. "It would me."

Manota sighed heavily. "She is right, Torak. If you, any of us, were to show up at the dinner without the females Tai Tek would become suspicious. It would be too obvious we are planning something. He would never expect us to let our women be where there is possible danger."

"Then it is decided. The females will stay and participate in the trap," Ajaska said.

The three brothers nodded, their faces showing the pain such a decision cost them. Jazin looked at Star with barely concealed fury. She was too small, too delicate to be fighting. He should just take her off somewhere safe and...

"Jazin," Star said softly, pulling him from his thoughts.

"Yes, love."

"It's not going to happen, so don't even think of trying," Star murmured firmly.

Jazin sighed heavily again. "Yes, love."

The rest of the afternoon was spent planning what the women's roles would be during the dinner. They would be mingling with the other guests and acting as an extra set of eyes. The men hoped they would be ignored since they were female, even though they were considered female warriors. At no time would they leave the main room, unless accompanied by one of the men or one of the select elite force members.

Before leaving in the early evening, Star pulled River to one side. "I've been working on more clothing. I have special 'gowns' we can wear." She smiled mischievously when she noticed Torak looking at her.

"You are not planning anything, are you?" Jazin asked suspiciously when he caught Torak's look.

"Why would you think that?" Star asked as she looked up at him with an innocent smile.

Jazin looked at her a moment before groaning. *What have I ever done to deserve a woman like this?* he thought with a sense of foreboding.

* * *

As the days got closer to the dinner the men spent more time away, giving the girls more time together. River took Jo and Star down to the training room where they practiced intensely. Two of the new elite force members were assigned to watch them as Kev Mul Kar was busy finalizing plans with other members who would form the tighter core group of first responders.

Both men watched in appreciative silence as all three females worked out. After stretching, they would flow through all the obstacle courses, moving silently up and over walls, across beams, and down ropes, sometimes upside down, other times, pausing halfway before doing a flip and landing on silent feet on the mats below before coming up with a weapon in their hand to strike out at an imaginary opponent.

It was only when the females started practicing with the weapons that the men paled. Today, River and Star were practicing a routine River's parents had been famous for.

The men watched as Star pulled a compact crossbow off her waist, flipped a release to open it, and loaded six arrows into it, shooting them at River in rapid succession. River dodged them, bending, rolling, and twirling at the last second before the last one came at her. The men heard Star gasp, watching in horror as the last arrow came at River's chest as she was turning away from the last one. The men started running. They yelled into a com device as they charged toward River.

Within minutes Torak, Jazin, and Manota were rushing into the training room. They found River on the floor next to the two elite force members, Star and Jo stood over them

"Breathe, okay. Just put your heads between your knees and take a steady breath. You'll be okay. The dizziness will pass," Torak heard Jo say softly.

"What in the name of all the gods and goddesses happened?" Torak roared, paling as he saw both men sitting on the floor with their heads between their knees. River was patting them gently on the back.

"It's okay, Torak. They'll be all right in a few minutes once the dizziness passes," River said, looking up while she continued rubbing the men's backs.

"You okay, honey?" Star asked one of the men who looked like he was about to pass out again.

"Honey?" Jazin growled. "You call him honey, while all I get is called—"

Star blushed. "Not now. Quit being such a jerk. I'm just trying to make him feel better."

"Jerk," Jazin stuttered. "She wants to make him feel better, and I get called a jerk for being worried out of my mind!"

Jazin pulled the hair on each side of his head before letting out a loud roar that resounded off the walls. Jazin glared at Star for a moment before walking with slow, determined steps toward her. Jazin gripped Star's wrist, glaring down at her.

"Enough, Star. You are mine. I am going to do something I should have done long ago. Computer, record: I, Jazin Ja Kel Coradon of the Third House of Kassis, claim you, Star, for my house and as my mate. I claim you as my woman. No other may claim you. I will kill any other who try. I give you my protection as is my right as leader of my house. I claim you as is my right by the House of Kassis. Computer, end recording and file." Without another word he swung Star into his arms, turned, and stormed out of the training room, leaving everyone behind them standing in stunned silence.

"Well, of all the nerve," Jo said sputtering. "Just who in the hell does he think he is?"

Manota glared at Jo. Jo, seeing the look on his face, stumbled backward, holding up her palms.

"Now, don't you go getting any ideas! I already told you it wasn't happening." Jo let out a squeal and turned to run only to be grabbed from behind and swung her over his shoulder.

Growling, Manota started speaking, drowning out Jo's protests. "I claim you, Jo. I should have done it weeks ago. You are mine. Let it be known I, Manota Ja Kel Coradon of the Second House of Kassis, claim you, Jo, for my house and as my mate." Jo struggled, kicking out at Manota. She let out a howl of rage when he slapped her ass hard. "I claim you as my woman." He slapped her ass again when she didn't stop struggling. "No other may claim you." Slap. "I will kill any other who try." Slap. "I give you my protection as is my right as leader of my house." Slap. "I claim you as is my right by the House of Kassis."

By the fifth slap Jo had quieted down, her ass burning and her pussy wet. Manota growled again when Jo tried to speak, rubbing his hand on her burning ass. Jo stiffened for a moment before relaxing over his shoulder, not fighting any more.

Torak and River stared in disbelief as Manota turned and carried a quiet Jo out of the training room. It was only the groan from one of the men as he struggled to his feet that drew Torak's attention back to the matter at hand. The other man was still sitting on the mat looking only slightly better.

"What happened?" Torak demanded from between clenched teeth.

He had a bad feeling about what he was about to learn. He held his hand up when River tried to explain, holding his hand out instead for the data screen attached to the man's waist. The man silently handed it to Torak, giving River an apologetic look.

Torak watched the replay for a while. River knew exactly when he got to the part that had caused both men to almost pass out. River and Star were practicing a move River's dad had perfected with her mom. It was extremely dangerous. River's dad would shoot arrows or throw knives at her mother. Her mother would either dodge them or, as in this case, catch them at the very last second.

It took incredible discipline and concentration, not to mention someone you trusted. Everything was timed to perfection. River had heard Star's gasp and knew it was the one she was supposed to catch before it pierced her. Just to be on the safe side, they had been using rubber arrows. While it wouldn't have killed River if it had hit her, the arrow would have hurt like hell and left a bad bruise. River made sure not to get hit after she had been hit a number of times when practicing the routine with her dad.

Torak was extremely pale as he watched the vidcom of Star shooting the arrows at River and River dodging them until the last one. He turned almost white as the two men had when they had rushed to River. When she had turned, it looked like the arrow was embedded in her chest.

When they saw her pull the arrow away grinning and spinning it between her fingers, both of the men had almost passed out. Torak held his palm up, silencing the man. He calmly handed the data screen back to the man before he turned to River with no expression on his face.

"Torak," River said, reaching out to him.

"Not now. Not here," Torak said in a voice devoid of all emotion. "Go to our living quarters."

"I need to get—" River began.

Torak closed his eyes. "Go to our living quarters now, River."

River looked at the strained expression on Torak's face before nodding. She murmured a soft apology to the two guards for scaring them before hurrying out of the training room. She began running as soon as she was in the outside corridors. She made it back to their living quarters in record time, slamming the outer door as she walked through it.

Fear had turned to anger. What did she have to apologize for? What did any of them have to apologize for? They were only doing stuff they had been doing all their lives. It wasn't like those were even real arrows. She wasn't stupid! Her dad had told her to never use real ones because anyone could have a bad day. He had learned that the hard way when he had come close to killing her mother one time.

Pulling her clothes off, River headed for the bathroom. She was hot and sweaty from the workout and the run back to their living quarters. She took a moment to stretch while the water filled up the huge pool that worked as a tub. The water came from an underground stream heated by a thermal layer in the crust of the planet.

The water would be filtered then returned after her bath. She had fallen in love with it as she could practically swim in the huge pool while bathing. It also worked on the shower carved into the rock facing of the mountain the Houses of Kassis sat on. She would soak for a while to ease her muscles and her mind before confronting Torak. She wasn't going to apologize, she just wasn't! If she started apologizing now she would spend the rest of her life apologizing for everything she did.

Stepping into the warm water, River couldn't keep the groan of pleasure from escaping her lips. Diving into the water, she let it flow over her. She rolled over onto her back and closed her eyes, floating and letting the warm water soothe her as it moved around her body, caressing her in its gentle flow.

* * *

Torak paused in the doorway of the bathroom watching River as she floated in the water, her hands moving slowly back and forth while the water caressed her body. He had come close to joining the men on the mat when he watched the vidcom of the incident earlier.

He had flashbacks of her with blood dripping from her chest, collapsing in a puddle of blood next to him while he screamed for help. Torak began pulling the ties holding his shirt; shrugging out of it, his boots and pants quickly followed. He stepped into the warm water, swimming over to where River was floating.

River started when she felt hands slide under her. Opening her eyes, she stared into Torak's dark eyes drowning in the desperate desire she saw there. Lifting her arms, she moved into his arms, letting her legs move around his waist. Without a word, Torak slid into River, pulling her tightly against him as he moved in and out, thrusting with increasing force.

River tightened her hold around Torak's neck, hanging on. Torak held River's hips, thrusting up, pushing into her deeper and deeper with each thrust. River knew deep down something inside Torak had snapped. His fear had taken him beyond the point of rational thought, and he was acting on a primal urge to dominate her.

To show her she belonged to him, and he could not lose her, to anyone or anything. River felt her climax building as Torak pushed deeper, hitting every nerve ending inside her as he moved to claim her. When it peaked, River bucked, trying to get away from the overwhelming feelings flooding through her body. Screaming, she fought as Torak grimly held her tightly against him, not letting her move away from the source of her pleasure/pain. River felt his body tense before he let his own release flow into her hotly.

River collapsed against Torak. She was shocked when he suddenly pulled away from her and climbed out of the pool. River watched him fearfully. He had his back to her and still hadn't said a word. It was the silence which frightened her the most. Normally when he was mad at her he would yell or tell her she couldn't do something. Never had he just not said anything.

River watched as he picked up a towel and walked into the bedroom. She slowly climbed out of the pool, picking up a towel and blotting the water from her hair before wrapping the towel around her body. She nervously picked up a brush and followed Torak into the bedroom. Torak had dressed and was walking out of the room when she came in.

"Where are you going?" River asked quietly.

"There are things I must take care of. I will return later. Do not wait up for me," Torak replied without turning around. A moment later River heard the door to their living quarters close.

Chapter 18

It was the night before the dinner and Torak still barely talked to River, only answering direct questions with the least amount of words. River was a nervous wreck. She had not been allowed out of their living quarters.

Jo and Star had not been heard from since their last fateful day in the training room. The two elite guard members who had been at the training center had been replaced with two others who looked like they had eaten a lot of sour lemons. Every time she had tried to leave their living quarters the warriors had stood in front of her silently shaking their heads. By order of Lord Torak, River was to stay inside, they told her. They would gently push her back in and close the door.

River had tried at first to get a rise out of Torak, but he had remained silent turning and leaving. When he had returned, River had been asleep. She had woken to find herself being made exquisite love too. She had screamed out her release as she felt Torak pulse his own deep inside her.

Afterward, he had pulled out of her and left her again, returning after she had fallen into an exhausted sleep from crying. When she had woken in the morning he made love to her again. Afterward, he had pulled out of her arms, ignoring her cry to stay for just a little while.

This had been going on for three days, although it seemed more like a lifetime. River hadn't been sleeping well and had lost her appetite. This morning had been the last straw. She couldn't continue like this. The silence between them was killing her. She knew he enjoyed the sex as he came to her several times a day, making love to her without saying a word and leaving as soon as they had both found release. Her heart was breaking, and she didn't know what to do. She had no one to talk to. He wouldn't let her out of their living quarters, and apparently Jazin and Manota were not letting Star and Jo out either.

River knew she had to do one of two things — break the wall between them or give up. It hadn't helped that for the past two days she had been very nauseated when she had gotten up. She figured the stress of everything was finally getting to her.

Wiping a tear from her cheek, she decided she would play out her part tomorrow night at the dinner, then present Torak with an ultimatum: talk to her or let her go. She was slowly shattering into little pieces, not knowing what to do. River swayed taking deep breaths as another wave of nausea washed over her. Placing a hand to her stomach, she turned, heading for the bathroom.

Maybe a shower would help her feel better. She had only made it halfway through the bedroom when she was struck with a wave of dizziness that clouded her vision. She tried to make it back to the bed, but another wave struck her and darkness descended like a blanket, closing in around her falling form.

* * *

Torak sighed, throwing the data screen he was holding across the desk. He had been holding the damn thing for the past hour and couldn't have told a single person what was on it. He hated the silence between him and River.

At first he had just been too angry to talk. He had made love to her in the bathing pool, his body desperate to know she was okay. He had to leave right after that because he would have taken her again and again. He could feel himself losing control as the fear he felt at almost losing her again washed through him with such violence, it had almost felt physical. He didn't want to hurt her.

Afterward, he had wanted to punish her. It broke his heart when he came to bed and saw the evidence of her tears on her face or heard her plead with him to stay and hold her after they had made love. He couldn't stay with her, but he couldn't stay away from her.

Groaning, he felt his body stir again as he remembered the feel of her sweet body wrapped around his this morning. She was so responsive to his touch. Getting up, he gave a disgusted groan. He wanted—no, needed—her again. He had taken her over and over the past few days, thinking he could work her out of his system. He had even thought for a brief moment to go to another female for relief, to see if that would help, but he couldn't imagine touching another.

Moving with purpose, he opened the door to the planning room and headed toward his living quarters. He would take her again. She was his mate. He had claimed her, and he wanted her.

Why shouldn't I take what is mine? He thought with a growl. Besides, it wasn't like she didn't enjoy it. Every time they came together, she was wild and willing in his arms.

Nodding at the two guards who moved aside quietly, he opened and closed the door softly. Glancing around the room, he frowned when he saw the uneaten food on the table. The past couple of mornings he had made sure River had been sent food. The past two days it had been returned uneaten.

Surely, she was up by now, Torak thought with a frown. Perhaps, she was in the shower or the bathing pool. She seemed to like both of those lately. They had made love in both of them many times since he had claimed her.

Moving toward the bedroom, he frowned when he saw the windows were still shaded. Giving the command to lighten them so natural light could pour into the room, Torak gave a cry of alarm when he saw River lying in a crumpled heap next to the bed. Rushing to her, he gently rolled her over, brushing her hair away from her face with a trembling hand. She was deathly pale, her dark lashes lying so still on her pale cheeks.

"River, little one, talk to me," Torak begged.

He picked her up and laid her on the bed. Pulling a com from his waist, he spoke quickly, requesting the healer to come to his living quarters immediately. River didn't move as Torak laid her down or when he covered her gently. Feeling her forehead and cheeks, he noted they seemed cool and clammy to his touch.

He almost growled when one of his guards knocked on the bedroom door.

"The healer, my lord," the guard said, looking with concern at River.

The elderly healer who had attended River when she had been shot walked into the room just as River let out a small moan. Torak spun around and clutched River's small hand in his larger one.

"Little one, look at me," Torak murmured, running a shaking hand over her pale face.

"What is wrong with her?" Torak demanded hoarsely as he glared at the healer.

"I am not sure. Can you tell me what happened?" The healer moved over to the bed and placed his hand on River's head. River opened her eyes. She stared up at Torak with cloudy, confused eyes.

"Torak?" River said weakly.

"I came in and found her unconscious on the floor. She is just now waking up. I do not know how long she was unconscious," Torak said tensely.

The healer looked at Torak for a moment before turning to look down at River. "If you wouldn't mind stepping into the other room, I'll examine her. I will be out shortly."

Torak looked like he was about to protest, but the healer smiled gently. "Go have a drink, my lord. I believe it will help."

Torak looked undecided for a moment before nodding and slowly standing up. He started to turn but stopped at the last moment to bend and brush a light kiss over River's lips before he left.

"I'll give you ten minutes. Then I am coming back," Torak said as he pulled the door closed.

River looked up at the healer in confusion. She didn't remember anything but feeling a little nauseated and dizzy. She watched as the healer pulled a scanner out of his bag and pulled the covers back. He ran the scan over her several times before he gently touched her stomach, pressing on it gently. After a couple of minutes, he pulled the covers back over her and put his scanner away.

"Well?" River asked, scared. "Do you know what's wrong with me?"

The healer smiled gently. He loved it when he was right. "Yes, my dear. You are expecting your first child. Would you like to know if it is going to be a boy or a girl?"

River stared at the healer in disbelief, her hands moving protectively over her stomach. Her mind was in a whirlpool, spinning as she absorbed what the healer was saying.

"You can tell so soon?" She whispered.

"Of course. I would say you are almost two months along. You must have bred not long after you were shot," the healer said with an amused smile.

"What..." River started trying to talk over the lump in her throat. She didn't care if she was having a girl or a boy but to know so she could get ready would be nice. "What is it?"

"You are going to have a very healthy boy from the looks on the scan. I took the liberty of completing some additional tests while you were in the medical wing and made sure there would be no compatibility issues between our species and yours. There are a few differences, but our bloods are tolerant of each other. You should not have any difficulty as far as that is concerned. Our gestation period is eight and a half months. Can you tell me what the normal time period is for your species?"

"Nine months," River whispered. She was going to have a baby boy, Torak's son.

"That is good. I would like to see you in a few days to do a complete work-up and prescribe you some vitamins to take. Your blood pressure is up a little, and I would like to make sure you eat properly and avoid stressful situations. You may exercise, but I caution using common sense and to keep it less strenuous than what you are normally accustomed to." The healer was just finishing his instructions when the door slammed back. Torak came in followed by his brothers, Jo, Star, Ajaska, and the two guards. The healer turned as everyone crowded into the room. Giving Torak a stern look, the healer addressed him.

"She must not be upset in any way. I want to see her again in a few days to run a complete series of tests. I want her to rest today. Make sure she eats. Several small meals at frequent intervals throughout the day would be best. She needs to build her strength. I will prescribe her additional supplements after I have run all the tests. She may exercise, but she must keep it light. Congratulations, my lord. Your Grace, congratulations," the healer said as he picked up his bag and walked past everyone who stood looking at him.

"Congratulations?" Torak said, confused. Jo and Star looked at each other for a minute before they let out a squeal of delight and flew to the bed.

"Oh, we're going to be aunts!" They pulled River into their arms, hugging her. "Oh, River, we are so happy for you. When Jazin and Manota heard the frantic call for the healer we made them bring us to make sure you were okay. Oh, honey, you are going to be a beautiful mother."

"Mother?" Torak said, standing there stupidly looking at River, Jo, and Star.

Jazin came up and patted Torak on the back. "Congratulations, brother," Jazin walked over and pulled a reluctant Star off the bed, murmuring softly in her ear before leaving the room.

"Congratulations, Torak," Manota grinned. "Perhaps now she will calm down," he said as he turned to look at Jo. He gave her a speculative look before he grinned. "Perhaps you have the right idea."

Jo shot Manota a dirty look and climbed off the bed. "Don't get any ideas," she muttered as she walked toward the door.

"Yes, I believe you may have the right idea," Manota murmured softly before patting his brother on the back and following his reluctant mate out the door.

Ajaska walked over to where River was leaning against the pillows. He leaned down and gently kissed her on her forehead. "I am proud to call you daughter. I look forward to seeing my son's child grow within you. It will be as beautiful as its mother."

"He." River smiled up with tears glittering in her eyes. "It's a boy."

"I look forward to seeing my son's son grow within his beautiful mother," Ajaska said, bowing to River before looking sternly at his son. "I expect you to care for her right. I will be most displeased if she is upset at all!"

"A boy?" Torak said blankly, staring at his father with unfocused eyes.

Ajaska just laughed as he took in his son's stunned face. Nodding to the two guards who waited patiently at the door, he looked one last time at River, winking before he left. The room seemed strangely quiet with just her and Torak there. River ran one hand protectively over her stomach while the other played nervously with the covers.

"Are you disappointed?" River asked in a barely audible voice, unable to look at Torak.

She was afraid. She wasn't sure what she would do if he was. She would figure something out. After the last few days, she just wasn't sure of anything anymore. A tear slipped out and slid slowly down her cheek when Torak didn't answer. River felt the bed dip as Torak sat down next to her.

"Hush, little one. How can I be disappointed when it is something I have dreamed about since the first time I saw you on the Tearnat's warship? I dreamed of how beautiful you would be rounded with my child. I crave the sight of my son or daughter suckling at your breasts. I love you, River. I have from the first time I saw you," Torak said softly, sincerely.

River looked up, her deep dark blue eyes glittering with unshed tears. "I love you, too. I've been so scared you didn't love me anymore. I didn't know what to do." River buried her face in his neck holding him close. "Oh Torak, I love you so much."

Torak gently wiped the tears from her cheeks brushing his lips across hers. "You are mine, River, forever. I, Torak Ja Kel Coradon of the Lead House of Kassis, claim you, River, for my House and as my mate. I claim you as my woman. No other may claim you. I will kill any other who try. I give you my protection as is my right as leader of my House. I claim you as is my right by the House of Kassis. I am proud to call you mother of my children and will love you forever."

Chapter 19

The night of the dinner was finally upon them. All the plans were in place, including a few modifications to River's plans. Torak was beside himself with the idea of her being in danger. After she had fainted the day before he had insisted she stay in bed all day. He had spent a good portion of the day in it with her, but refused to make love to her again until the healer said it would be all right.

River had been so beside herself by late afternoon she had made Torak contact the healer, who had assured him making love would not endanger River or the baby and would, by all accounts, be a positive way to keep River relaxed and less stressed. Torak had barely acknowledged the healer's final comment before he hung up the com and had River pinned to the bed under him. He had fed her every couple of hours until she laughingly told him she couldn't eat another bite. That was before he had offered himself for dessert. She decided she always had room for him and had taken him to new heights with his cries resounding off the walls of their bedroom.

This morning he had carried her to the bathroom and bathed her. They had ended up making love again in the shower. River couldn't help but laugh at Torak's insistence to baby her. She let him. She figured in a few days she was going to have to enlist the help of his brothers and father to rescue her before he drove her insane, but, until then, she just wanted to enjoy all the attention he was lavishing on her. She had never felt so loved, so needed, so beautiful in all her life.

Now, as she prepared for the dinner her hand moved to lie over her stomach protectively as she adjusted the knife she had strapped to the inside of her arm. She would have to be extra careful from now on as there was more than just herself to consider. She was wearing the special gown Star had designed for her. The top was low cut and showed a significant amount of cleavage. Star had explained it would help with the distraction and give the impression of being more feminine, camouflaging her warrior image as the men had difficulty thinking warriors could have boobs.

River had just laughed, but she had to agree her breasts were fuller than they had been before, so she was definitely showing her feminine side. The skirt part of it was really a pair of pants with the outer layer, giving the appearance of a long, full skirt. It could be detached in less than a second to give freedom of movement.

There were several hidden slits that were open on both the insides of her sleeves and the pants. Each one had a sheath that matched the color of the outfit making it more difficult to see. Inside were a collection of knives. Her belt was a beautiful collection of glowing, jeweled stars which were actually made of crystal. Each one could be detached and used as a throwing star, the hard crystal making it a perfect weapon.

The last weapon was discretely hidden in River's hairpiece. Twin hairpins were really throwing knives. They were sheathed in beautifully carved crystal to match her belt. River felt like Star had missed her calling. She should have been working for the government designing outfits for their spies. James Bond was never as well prepared as River was tonight.

River turned as Torak came into the room. She gazed at him, her love for him shining like twin beacons of light from her dark blue eyes. He was breathtakingly handsome in his uniform. It was solid black with gold braids embroidered on each shoulder.

He wore a white shirt under his snug-fitting jacket which tapered at the waist. His pants looked like they could have been painted on him, they fit his form so well and were tucked into a pair of shiny knee-high black boots. He wore a decorative battle sword on one hip and a small laser pistol on the other. His thick long hair was pulled back and tied.

"You are so handsome," River breathed as she glided across the room to him.

"And you are the most beautiful creature I have ever laid eyes upon," Torak replied, bringing River's hands up to his mouth and kissing the backs of them gently.

"You remember what you are supposed to do?" Torak asked gently as he drew River into his arms.

"Yes," River said with a small laugh. "Keep my eyes open and stay out of trouble."

"And stay safe. For me, little one, and for our son, you must not do anything that will endanger either one of you," Torak murmured into her hair, his grip tightening around her.

"I promise," River said softly, pulling back and looking up into Torak's eyes. She stood on her tiptoes and gave him a light kiss on the lips just as a knock sounded at door of their living quarters.

* * *

River walked safely surrounded by Torak on one side and his father on the other. They met up with Jazin and Star and Manota and Jo in the center of the garden. It was a beautiful night, and the stars were beginning to come out. All three girls gasped as they saw the twin moons.

"It's so beautiful," River said in a hushed voice, looking up.

The moons came into orbit together approximately every ninety days. This was the first they had aligned since River, Jo, and Star had been on Kassis. They looked so huge in the early evening sky.

Torak and Ajaska just grinned down at River, enjoying her awed expression at something they took for granted. Torak felt like everything else paled in comparison to River's beauty. Since she'd found out she was with child, she seemed to glow as brightly as the moons she looked upon.

Letting his hand slide around to the small of her back, he couldn't help the wicked smile that curved his lips at her response to his touch. He would be glad when the evening was concluded so he could return her to the safety of their House and his bed.

The three couples and Ajaska climbed the stairs to the rear entrance of the South House and moved into position. Jo and Star winked at River as they walked by with a softly muttered, "Showtime," under their breath. River barely bit back the laugh that threatened to escape. Even so, Torak sent her a dark look that spoke of his suspicion the girls were up to something.

Ajaska and Torak moved to greet people at the front entrance as they began arriving. River, Jo, and Star were to meet in the large ballroom where people would be mingling, enjoying light refreshments before the dinner and additional entertainment afterward. Jo would go with Manota first to meet with the elite team covering the kitchens, while Star went with Jazin to meet with the team covering the upstairs. River highly suspected it was the men's way of trying to keep the three of them from getting together any sooner than necessary.

River picked up a non-alcoholic drink and sipped it, enjoying the cool, refreshing taste of the fruit juice. She wandered over to the double doors leading out onto the terrace and looked out over the gardens. Tonight would be interesting. They would either catch Tai Tek in their trap, or he would get away once again. He reminded River of a slippery eel hiding in wait for an unsuspecting victim.

"It's quite enchanting, it is not?" a soft voice said behind her.

River froze for a moment before relaxing. "Yes, it is." A small smile curved her lips. "I'm so sorry about scaring your men the other day."

Kev Mul Kar gave a husky laugh as he replied. "Yes. The other men were having a great time teasing them until they saw the vidcom of your little stunt. I think all of them became very sympathetic when Borat and Waytec were assigned to you. I wish you congratulations on your breeding. Motherhood is very becoming on you," Kev Mul Kar added softly, studying the glow on River's face.

It was true—River did seem to glow with a radiance that softened her face and gave her an air of fragile elegance.

River glanced over her shoulder at Kev Mul Kar, blushing. "Thank you."

Kev Mul Kar cleared his throat before he continued. "Please remember to stay in either this room or the dining room at all times. Do not leave either for any reason. Someone will be watching you at all time."

River rolled her eyes at Mul Kar and stuck out her tongue just enough for him to see the pink tip of it. It took everything Mul Kar had not to groan at the innocent gesture. "You have been talking to Torak."

Mul Kar couldn't have responded if he wanted to. His throat had suddenly closed over the lump in it. With a stiff nod, he moved away. Jo and Star had just walked into the room and watched as he moved by them, giving them a quick bow.

"What got his panty hose in a bind?" Jo asked, puzzled, as they came up to River.

Star just rolled her eyes at River. "You know, for being the oldest you are not always the brightest bulb in the package. Can't you tell he is half in love with River? He has been since the Tearnat's warship."

River looked at Star like she had lost her mind. "What? Don't tell me you didn't know that either?" Star asked. "And you guys think I'm naive!"

"So, what's the plan?" Jo asked, looking around at the people coming in.

There were dignitaries from all the different provinces, as well as intergalactic members. River's eyes darkened with sorrow when she saw Gril Tal Mod enter the room along with a female version of their species. She still had trouble accepting she had killed his son, no matter if he had been about to execute his own father. Murmuring a brief excuse to Jo and Star, River moved over to greet the Tearnat leader.

"Lord Tal Mod?" River called out softly. She wasn't sure on how to address him as she had never had to formally greet intergalactic leaders before.

Gril Tal Mod turned to see River approaching him. His gaze missed nothing as it flowed over her figure in the gown Star had created. She looked far different than the warrior woman she had appeared to be on his warship.

"Lady River, a pleasure to see you again. Might I say you look even more beautiful than the last time we met. May I introduce my mate, Madas Tal Mod,"

Gril Tal Mod pulled his lips back in what resembled a smile for his species showing an expanse of long, sharp teeth.

River felt a moment of horror at the idea this was Trolis' mother. What must she think of River? Gril Tal Mod watched curiously as River's eyes darkened with sadness at the reminder, and her eyes filled with unshed tears.

"I just wanted to welcome you tonight. It is good to see you as well," River replied softly, looking at the female who had been regarding the exchange with a curious expression on her face.

"You are the warrior woman my mate told me about?" the huge female hissed softly.

"Yes, Lady Tal Mod. I wish to convey my regret at the death of your son," River replied, standing up straight.

"You must call me Madas. I am not much for titles as my mate will tell you. Our son deserved worse. You gave him a more peaceful death than he deserved for all he did. I wish to thank you for saving the life of my mate. You have nothing to regret. I would have killed Trolis myself if I had been there," the female hissed, placing her hand on Gril Tal Mod's. "My mate is my life. You have protected him. We will always be in your debt."

River was stunned to hear Gril Tal Mod's mate talk so distastefully about her late son. Madas stepped forward, taking one of River's small hands in her large, scaled one and looking almost amused as she watched the emotions chase across River's face.

Turning to look at her mate, Madas asked teasingly, "Gril, are you sure she is a warrior? She is so delicate and small. How can something so tiny bring your great warship to a standstill? Perhaps you should offer her a position training your warriors."

River looked up into Madas' face and watched as slowly one lid came down over her large eye. *She just winked at me*, River thought in disbelief.

Giggling, River responded lightheartedly. "I would love to show his warriors some moves. I hope his warriors can handle it better than Torak's! They have a tendency to pass out or hyperventilate when we girls are around."

Gril Tal Mod hissed at his mate, pulling her back against him, wrapping his arm around her, "You will pay for your insolence later, Madas."

"Promises, promises," Madas hissed back, looking at River with a twinkle in her large eyes before they moved away.

* * *

"Okay, that was just creepy," Jo said, watching the two Tearnats' nuzzle each other.

River's laugh died in her throat as she watched Grif Tai Tek walk into the room with none other than Javonna on his arm. River slid a hand protectively over her abdomen, trying to quell the sudden feeling of queasiness she was feeling.

"That bastard," Jo said under her breath.

"That bitch," Star's snarled vehemently. "I told Torak I'd kill that bitch if she ever came in the same room as you."

River and Jo turned to look at Star in disbelief. They had never heard her say anything so...so nastily before. She sounded like she fully intended to follow through. River felt a small giggle escape, followed by another one until she was laughing out loud. Only Star could make her feel better about seeing Torak's ex-lover in the same room. Now, River would spend the rest of the evening visualizing all the ways Star would slowly kill Javonna.

"Oh, Star, I love you," River said as she slipped her hand into Star's, giving it an appreciative squeeze.

Chapter 20

Tai Tek looked at the three female warriors, barely able to hide his surprise at their transformation. If he had not been on the receiving end of the sword of the blue-eyed female he would never have believed they were warriors. The blue-eyed female glowed with a radiance that took his breath away and hardened his cock.

He wanted her. He would have her before the night was over. Once he had eliminated her mate, he would claim her for himself.

"I'm thirsty," Javonna muttered coldly under her breath, staring daggers at River.

Tai Tek looked down with distaste at Javonna. "Get yourself something to drink, then," he said as he turned with an air of dismissal that infuriated Javonna as she watched him walk toward Torak's mate.

"My dear Lady River, you make the moons of Kassis pale in comparison to your beauty," Tai Tek said as he bowed slightly to River. His eyes barely acknowledged Jo and Star standing slightly behind her.

River looked at Tai Tek with a slightly wary look. "Lord Tai Tek, it is good to know you do not hold grudges. I hope you enjoy the dinner. It is my understanding it is a celebration of a new trade agreement."

Tai Tek looked into River's eyes before smiling slightly. "How could I hold bad feelings against someone as lovely as you? If I had not seen, with my own eyes— and felt—your skills, my lady, I would find it hard to believe you are the same woman who held a sword to my throat."

Oops, thought River. *He still holds a grudge.*

River smiled, slightly amused at the veiled reminder. "You have to admit it was a grand entrance. If you will excuse me, Lord Tai Tek, I believe my husband—ah, mate—has finished with his duties." River nodded her head in a regal bow of dismissal and moved with shaking knees toward Torak who had just entered the room.

Tai Tek watched as River, followed by Jo and Star, moved away from him. He let a small cruel smile curve his lips for a moment before his face returned to the bland mask he kept for functions such as this. Soon, Torak, his father, and two brothers would be dead.

He had planned well. The Tearnat would be suspected of their murders, done in revenge for killing his second son. He would get rid of the oversized reptile at the same time as he eliminated the leading members of Kassis and the House of Kassis.

Then, he would claim the female warriors as his. He would keep the blue-eyed warrior for his own until he tired of her. He would give the other two to his loyal guards who would share them among themselves before killing them. He suspected the little warriors wouldn't last long.

Turning when he felt nails digging into his arm, Tai Tek looked down at Javonna with a dark smile. "You are ready, my dear. I know how hurt you were by the blue-eyed warrior's replacement of you. Bring her to me and Torak will be all yours."

Javonna watched as Torak put his arm around River, pulling her close. A savage smile curled her lips before she softly replied, "I'll bring her to you, my lord. I promise, before the night is over, I will bring her to you and you can do whatever you want with her."

* * *

Torak's eyes narrowed as he noticed Tai Tek talking to River. It took all of his willpower to force himself to remain calm. He would have cut the man in half right where he stood if River hadn't turned and looked at him with an amused gleam in her eye.

She took his breath away. When Tai Tek had walked through the doors with Javonna on his arm, Torak had barely contained his fury. He did not want River upset and knew she would be when she saw Javonna there. He had wanted to go seek her out immediately, but couldn't leave his duties. Gritting his teeth, he thought of nothing else while he stood helplessly greeting guests, but how hurt and upset River must be.

"I thought you would be in a much different mood," Torak said softly as he pulled River into his arms. "I had no idea he would bring her tonight. If I had, I would have prevented it somehow."

River laughed softly as she stood on her tiptoes to brush a kiss across Torak's mouth. "Relax, Star has it covered. I'm going to be spending the rest of the evening imagining how many ways she is going to kill Javonna. It will actually give us something to do and be fun."

"I love you, River. Remember that. I have claimed you as mine," Torak murmured, kissing River more deeply.

"Humph," Ajaska said, clearing his throat loudly. "How can you keep your mind focused and your eyes clear if you have them glued to my new daughter?"

River laughed. "Go on. You two go socialize. I need to visit the little girl's room."

Torak and Ajaska looked puzzled. Both repeated with a frown, "Little girl's room?"

"I have to go to the bathroom to powder my nose. I'll take Jo and Star with me to cover my back." River laughed.

Torak watched as River spoke softly to Jo, then to Star. Both nodded and followed her out of the room. Torak knew there were guards everywhere, so he felt a little better about letting River Co. None of them expected Tai Tek to do anything until after the dinner. Torak felt a wave of unease flow through him suddenly, and he looked around until he met his Captain of the Guard's dark eyes. With a slight nod, Kev Mul Kar followed the women.

Picking up a drink from one of the passing servants, he started to take a sip when a scaly hand gently stopped him.

Startled, Torak looked up into the eyes of Madas Tal Mod who was hissing softly. "I don't believe the beverage would be suitable for your tastes, my lord.

May I recommend a beverage from a different servant's tray?"

Torak looked at the drink, his lips thinning into a straight line. "How did you know?"

Madas pulled back her lips showing an expanse of sharp teeth. "Your mate is not the only female warrior. I have a highly developed sense of smell for certain poisons native to our lands. I can smell the odor of the junta tree from across a room."

The junta tree only grew on the Tearnats' home planet, in a heavily wooded area where Madas Tol Mod's clan came from. A few sips of the drink and he would have been dead in a matter of moments. Once the cause was discovered it would be assumed Gril Tal Mod was behind his death. Torak looked around quickly for his brothers and father afraid they would have been offered the same poisoned drink.

"Do not worry. They have already been warned, and no others have been offered a drink. Gril is most displeased that someone would try to kill you and your family. He does not appreciate others trying to incriminate the Tearnats for murder. We do have some honor. If we want someone dead, we simply kill them," Madas hissed, amused. "The servant will be disposed of immediately."

Torak gave a tense nod at Madas. "My mate and her sisters?"

Madas hissed softly. "They were not offered a drink, I believe on purpose. Keep a close watch on them. I fear whoever is behind this has plans for your females."

* * *

River walked into the elaborately decorated bathroom. She couldn't help but laugh; everything about the House of Kassis was over the top. Moving over to the mirror, River checked her makeup while Star and Jo went to the bathroom. Suddenly, another image came into view behind River.

Javonna looked dispassionately at River, staring down at the smaller woman with a cruel twist to her lips. She moved over to the mirror as if checking her own makeup before saying anything. "You know he will tire of you soon."

River raised her eyebrow at Javonna and didn't say anything. What could she say? Quit being such a bitch? Get over it, already? Nothing she said would make a difference so she figured it wasn't worth wasting her breath.

"I want him back," Javonna continued. "I did well in his House. I was the lead lover and controlled all the other women. I knew how to satisfy him."

River's eyes darkened at the reminder of Javonna knowing Torak intimately. There was only so much she was willing to put up with and being reminded of Javonna in Torak's arms was not going to happen.

"Javonna, if you know what is good for you, you will stop right now," River said coldly.

Javonna turned to look down on River with distaste. "And who is going to stop me?"

Star and Jo came out from behind the wall separating the toilets from the washroom. "I will, you big bitch," Star said, looking up at Javonna. "I told

Torak if you were ever in the same room as River I would kill your ass, so if you don't want to die before dinner I suggest you get your bitchy self out of here."

River and Jo looked at Star in stunned silence. Star was the shortest and most petite out of all three of them, but at that moment she looked like she could not only open a can of whup-ass, she could close it too. Javonna looked down at Star for a moment before she backed up slowly, looking at all three of the women.

"You are brave when there are three of you together. It will be interesting to see how brave you are when you are alone," Javonna said before twirling around and moving quickly out the door.

Kev Mul Kar watched as Javonna brushed past him. He turned to River with concern when he saw her walk out of the restroom.

"All is well, my lady?" Kev asked softly.

River smiled at Kev before nodding. "Yes, Star took care of it. She told Javonna if she didn't want to die before dinner she'd better get her butt out of the way."

Kev Mul Kar looked at Star with startled eyes before letting out a quiet laugh. He would have liked to have seen the little warrior threaten Javonna. He had never liked that particular female.

* * *

Torak looked around for River, Jo, and Star. They were talking quietly with his father. River glanced over at Torak and smiled gently as she moved a protective hand over her stomach. A fierce wave of protectiveness swept through Torak. He had to get her to safety as soon as this was over.

Torak walked by Kev Mul Kar and handed him the glass. "Test this," he murmured without breaking stride, and headed for his mate.

"Torak, your father said someone tried to poison all of you. They are trying to kill not just you and your father but your brothers as well," River said with a shaky smile.

"Now they have just pissed me off," Jo said with a sharp nip in her tone. She was more than pissed; she was ready for some revenge. No one messed with those she loved. "Where is Manota?"

"He and Jazin will join us shortly," Torak said, looking warily at the three women. He had never seen all three of them mad at the same time, though he had been on the receiving end of one angry female. If the destruction they did to the Tearnat's warship was any indication of what they were like when they weren't mad, he couldn't imagine what they would do when they were.

"Madas seems to think they will not harm you or your sisters. Be careful. I do not like the way things are progressing," Torak said softly, bringing River's clenched fist to his mouth.

River shivered at the feel of Torak's firm lips against her hand. "Perhaps we should circulate separately. They may feel more confident to try something."

Torak's eyes flashed with fire. "You will not put yourself in danger."

River smiled and rested her palm on Torak's cheek. "Of course not. I'm simply going to make small talk and listen. I'll be in the same room as you."

Torak's eyes darkened with frustration and anger. It took everything in him not to call Tai Tek out. He watched as River moved to join a small group of women standing not far from him.

* * *

Javonna watched through narrowed eyes as River moved around the room. She was furious at Star's threat to her. She couldn't wait until the small human was spread beneath Tai Tek's men. She would ask to watch as they took her. It would be a just reward to watch her suffer.

She had to think of a way to get the warrior bitch, River, alone. It seemed as if she was always with the other two warrior women, Torak, or one of his guards. She looked speculatively at Kev Mul Kar. She knew he had never liked or trusted her. She had tried on several occasions to get rid of him, but he had always slipped through the traps she had set.

Now, she watched as his eyes never left River. A small, satisfied smile curved her lips. Perhaps, she had finally found a way to get rid of him.

Dinner passed without further interruptions. This made River very wary as she knew calm often came before the storm. River had developed an instant rapport with Madas. She listened to Madas tell tales of Gril's misadventures when he was courting her. It seemed they had more in common than River would have ever guessed.

Gril looked on with affection as his mate told the tales, at times refuting some of her claims to have driven him to distraction with some of her outlandish behaviors. Throughout the dinner, Torak would reach out to touch River, sometimes discretely, other times very blatantly. River never complained. She found it reassuring.

After dinner, the men would retire to one room and the women to another. River, Jo, and Star had stared at Torak, Manota, and Jazin like the men were out of their minds. It had to be the most antiquated practice they had ever heard of during their lifetimes.

..*

The men soon departed for their assigned entertainment while the women were escorted to theirs. River's face reflected her dour mood as she moved into the room clustered with the other women. Jo and Star obviously felt the same way from the look they gave her.

"I guess it is time to be the perfect little woman," Jo muttered under her breath, looking around at all the ladies. Except for Madas, they hadn't found any they could really relate to.

River let out a deep sigh as music began playing. It was some weird number they had never heard of, with unusual instruments playing. Star made a face before she put her finger in her mouth, mimicking being gagged.

River couldn't contain her soft laugh. "You girls go circulate. Keep your eyes and ears open for anything that might be useful."

Javonna gave a sigh of relief when she saw the three female warriors break up to move around the room to talk to other women in attendance. Grabbing a drink from a servant, she slid a vial out of her sleeve and emptied it into the drink. Walking toward River, she put on her sweetest smile.

"Lady River," Javonna said quietly. "A moment of your time, please."

River turned to look at Javonna. So, it was showtime, after all. River nodded her head slightly and followed Javonna over to a corner near the huge doors leading out into the gardens.

Javonna smiled and picked up another drink as a servant walked by. Holding out one to River, Javonna took a sip from the new glass. River took the glass from Javonna with a quiet, "Thank you."

"I believe I owe you an apology for my behavior. I have behaved in a most disgraceful manner. I do hope you will accept my sincere apology. It is hard when one is forced to leave the House they had sought for so long," Javonna said, sipping her drink again.

River let a small smile curve her lips. Raising the drink to her own lips she acted as if she was taking a sip from it. She had watched enough movies to know better than to ever take a drink from someone who wanted you dead, especially if that someone started apologizing to you.

"I'm sorry you were so hurt, Javonna. I never expected to fall in love with Torak and never expected him to fall in love with me. Where I come from it is normally one man and one woman. I am glad you understand there was no malicious intent," River said softly. Let the bitch take that to the bank. Two could play this game.

Javonna drained the rest of her drink before replying. "Yes, well, I wish you long life."

"Thank you, Javonna. Long life to you, too," River said politely, not meaning a word of it.

Acting like she was taking another drink, River waited until Javonna looked at Star and Jo walking toward them before she discretely poured the rest of the drink in a nearby plant. When Javonna turned to look at her again, it looked like she had just finished the drink. River handed the empty glass to a nearby servant.

"If you will excuse me, Javonna," River said, turning to look at Star and Jo.

"Of course, my lady," Javonna said with a broad smile. Javonna walked by Star and Jo, giving both of them a smile as she moved into the crowd of ladies.

"What was that all about?" Jo asked suspiciously.

"The bitch must not watch American television very often. I'll bet you a hundred dollars she tried to give me a doped-up drink," River murmured.

"So, how do we prove it?" Star asked, watching Javonna move across the room.

"It's showtime, girls. I have a feeling shit is about to hit the fan. I am going to act like I suddenly don't feel well. You ready?" River asked quietly.

Both Jo and Star grinned. "Oh, I love a great performance."

River groaned softly, placing one hand on her stomach and one on her head. Swaying she let her knees bend. Jo and Star reached to grab her as she collapsed. Moaning, River let her head drop back on her shoulders.

"Help, someone help!" Star called out frantically. "River, oh River, are you okay?"

River just moaned and let her eyes close as Jo and Star carefully lowered her to the floor. The women in the room started calling out for help. Almost immediately, two uniformed men approached.

"Lady River, what seems to be the problem?" One of the men asked kneeling next to River.

River moaned, barely opening her eyes so she could look at the man. The digital reading from her contact lens told her it was not one of their security men, even though he was wearing a uniform. Manota had made sure all the members of the security team were programmed into the database in the lens.

River looked at Jo and Star shaking her head before moaning again. Speaking in Italian she mumbled. "These men are fakes."

The men looked at Jo and Star to see what River said.

"She must be out of her mind. She's mumbling nonsense," Jo said, letting tears fill her eyes. "Please, you have to help her."

"Move back. We will take her to medical. Both of you may follow us," the taller of the two men said. The one kneeling next to River bent and lifted her gently into his arms. River moaned again, letting one of her arms reach around behind the man while the other moved over his chest.

"Torak. Please, Torak," River whispered before closing her eyes.

Star began crying as the taller of the men placed his arm around her waist. Leaning on him, she sobbed as he escorted her and Jo out of the room. Jo moved to stand on the other side, walking so close she was practically touching him.

"She'll be all right, Star. You'll see, baby. River will be all right," Jo kept saying over and over as Star sobbed into the side of the one security guard.

Chapter 21

Torak stood near the doors of the huge room the men had been escorted to. He waited as his brothers and father moved into position as well. They would cover every exit to ensure Tai Tek did not escape.

As the performers filed onto a makeshift stage the lights lowered. Dozens of scantily clad women appeared on the stage and began dancing. Torak never took his eyes off Tai Tek.

"Do you have anything?" Torak asked Manota.

"Nothing yet. It shouldn't be long before the bastard tries something, though," Manota responded. "What about you, Jazin?"

"Nothing except if Star finds out about the women in here I will probably be dead by morning," Jazin said, letting his eyes roam over the crowd. "Several of the females are identified as belonging to Tai Tek's house. I am not sure I like this."

"I would not put it past him to threaten them with punishment if they did not do as he told them," Ajaska responded. "Manota. Can you identify the group of men who just entered through the east entrance? Those doors were sealed."

No sooner had the words left Ajaska's mouth than shouts and screams could be heard. Laser fire began filling the room as the group of men coming in through the east entrance started firing up at the ceiling, yelling for everyone to lie down. The dancers began screaming and tried to run for the door they had entered through only to be stunned before they could escape.

Several men in the front of the room took blasts to the chest, collapsing in a heap on the floor of the ballroom. Ajaska roared out, pulling his laser pistol and firing it at the men charging him. Moving to stand behind a huge pillar he fired a shot, hitting one man and knocking him down.

"Manota, where are Kev and his men?" Ajaska yelled into his com link.

"They are fighting a group of men who landed on the roof and another trying to gain entrance through the front. They have them contained and are on their way here," Manota responded as he came up behind two of the invaders and cut them down. "Shit, two unidentified men have entered the room with the women."

Torak was fighting three other intruders who had tried to circle around Jazin. Jazin had his hands full with two men. Ajaska, seeing two of his sons surrounded by men, let out a roar that shook the room. Gril Tal Mod's head jerked up, his nostrils flared with anger. He reached out his massive arms, gripping the man fighting him, and squeezed. The man fell limply at his feet. Turning, he bent his powerful legs and leaped onto the backs of the two men fighting Jazin, crushing them under his weight.

"Go to the females. My mate says the females have been taken," Gril Tal Mod growled.

Torak roared out in rage slamming his knife into one man's chest while kicking the knee out from another before slashing the other man's throat with a back swing of his blade. Jazin plunged his blade forward into the last man, growling as he searched for Star's location on the embedded map in the lens in his eye.

"Shit. Star is not with the other females," Jazin said looking around wildly for Tai Tek. "Where is Tai Tek? Where is the bastard?"

The other men in the room quickly helped to subdue the attackers. Ajaska and Gril Tal Mod came forward, shoving chairs and tables out of their way. Manota reached them just as they got to Jazin and Torak.

Torak grabbed one of the rebels by the neck in a stranglehold. "Where are they taking the females?" he demanded in a voice devoid of all emotion.

"It is too late," the rebel croaked, turning red as he struggled for a breath. "Tai Tek will have already mated to your female, and the other two have been given to the other guards as payment for their loyalty."

Torak gripped the man's neck so hard it snapped. He let the limp body fall to the floor. His eyes glowed with fury. He would kill Tai Tek and every man who had supported him. He closed his eyes focusing on the map and the tracking signal of his mate and her sisters.

His eyes snapped open, and an unholy light glittered from him as he snarled. "They are in the garden. They must have used the females to escape into it."

* * *

River lay limply in the guard's arms, moaning softly as she mumbled in Portuguese, "I think it is almost showtime, girls."

"Oh, River, we're almost to the center of the garden. We'll be at your House soon," Star cried out softly. She moved her hand around the waist of the soldier holding her and slid his laser pistol over to Jo, who put it in a hidden pocket of her skirt.

Jo had already lifted the other soldier's weapon and inserted a toy pistol that belonged to one of the children from Manota's house. She had been leaning on him most of the way, sobbing her eyes out.

Both Jo and Star gave a startled cry when the soldiers suddenly stopped near the center fountain. A dark figure appeared from beside it. As he pulled back the hood of his cloak, Tai Tek's hard face appeared.

He looked at the three women, River lying limp in his guard's arms and the two tear-stained faces of the other females. The guard closest to Jo grabbed her arm, while another guard came out of the shadows and gripped Star. Jo and Star pushed against their attackers, fighting to break the hold the men had on them.

"It appears these warrior women are not as strong as it was first thought." Tai Tek's mouth curved into a cruel smile.

The guard holding River stepped forward. "My lord, we have brought the females as you asked. Lady River drank the drink given to her by Javonna."

"Remember your promise to let me watch you take her. I also want to watch as your guards share the little one," Javonna said nastily, stepping out from behind Tai Tek.

"I'm afraid, my dear, your usefulness has come to an end. You may also enjoy the attentions of my guards until they tire of you," Tai Tek said coldly before pushing Javonna toward the two guards who had appeared.

"You can't do that! You promised me if I helped you I could have Torak. You promised I could watch as you mated to that bitch. You promised I could watch as your guards raped and killed that little bitch!" Jovanna screamed in anger.

Tai Tek looked at Jovanna before smiling. "I lied."

Jovanna started screaming and fighting the two men holding her until one of the men turned her, slapping her hard across the face. She collapsed between them, whimpering, as they pulled her toward Torak's House.

"My lord, our forces have been defeated. The lords of Kassis are moving this way. We must leave at once," one of the guards said softly.

"Fools! What of the charges that were set?" Tai Tek coldly looked at his Captain of the Guard.

"We did not have a chance to set them before the guards attacked," his Captain of the Guard replied in a dead voice.

"It is time to go. Take the females through the passageway to the shuttle waiting on the other side of the complex. By the time they find them it will be too late," Tai Tek said, turning to leave.

"Not so fast, asshole," River said just as she swung her fist into the nose of the guard holding her. The man dropped her as his nose shattered under her direct hit.

River twisted as she fell, landing on her feet and doing a flip to put distance between her and the other guards. Turning to kneel, she threw two knives into the men holding Jo and Star who did twin backflips taking them to land near River. Jo pulled one of the pistols, firing rapidly while Star reached for her crossbow.

"Move, move, move," River yelled as she pulled back behind the fountain. She threw a knife, cursing as it imbedded in Tai Tek's shoulder. She had aimed for his heart, but the bastard had turned at the last minute.

Jo and Star moved back into the dark shadows, covering River as she turned to run. She counted three down, but there had to have been at least eight, counting Tai Tek. Ripping the covering of her skirt off, she let it fall to the ground as a laser blast missed her head by less than an inch. She hit the ground, rolling before coming back up on her feet.

They hadn't been sure where Tai Tek was going to strike or where they would be taken if he did capture them. The fact it was the garden was probably a blessing as the three of them knew it fairly well. Moving fast, each of the women grabbed the hanging from one of the tall pillars encircling the garden and started climbing. They figured they would have a better view of what was happening on the ground and could move over most of the garden by air. The lenses Manota had given them gave them night vision. By River's estimation they had about thirty minutes left before the lenses dissolved.

Reaching the top of the pillar, River rolled over and lay flat as Jo and Star came up behind her. "You two okay?" River asked softly.

Jo whispered. "Yeah. I'm cool. Star, what about you?"

Star reached down, feeling the sticky wetness on her side. She held back a gasp as pain flashed through her. Biting her lip, she whispered faintly, "I think you two are going to have to do this one without me."

River's head came up as she heard the pain in Star's voice. "Shit, where are you hit?"

"No, baby, no. Star, no," Jo whispered desperately, trying to hold back a cry of anguish. She moved over the narrow surface of the pillar trying to get to Star.

"Left side," Star replied faintly. "I took a hit as we were running." She gasped softly as Jo tried to move her. "Jo don't, I... Tell Jazin... I love him."

Jo gripped Star's hand tightly. "You'll have to tell him that, Star. You have to hold on until we can get you down from here. Do you hear me? You have to hold on, baby."

Star smiled softly, looking up at the twin moons. "It's so beautiful."

Jo couldn't contain the cry that broke from her as Star's eyes closed. "No!"

River turned as she heard the sound of feet moving underneath them. "Stay with Star. Protect her and keep her alive until we can get her help."

Jo nodded silently, trying to stem the blood flowing from the wound on Star's side. "I will. You kill that bastard for me, River. You kill him."

River nodded. Moving out over the wire she had to focus all of her talents on keeping her balance. It was one thing to tightrope walk in broad daylight or under lights; it was another to do it with a night-vision lens. She moved silently, stopping only once when she saw men moving down underneath her.

She moved to the next pillar, keeping an eye open for her target. She wanted to take out Tai Tek. Kill the leader and you cut off his troops, at least she hoped so. She moved over to the next pillar. Looking down, she saw Tai Tek near the steps of Torak's House, Javonna held tightly against him. So, the bastard was going to leave his men to rot while he sneaked off.

River climbed down the vines, moving silently until she was close enough to jump. Landing in a crouch, she waited to see if she could hear anyone close. She could vaguely hear the men moving off to her left, but they were far enough away, she could make it to the House without being seen.

Running swiftly, she leaped up onto the railing surrounding the front entrance. She had a feeling she knew where they were heading. During her early days of exploring she had discovered a passageway under the training room. The door had been locked, but it had not been a problem for her to pick the lock.

She had discovered it led to a cave inside the mountain before coming out onto a rocky ledge and a waterfall under the House of Kassis. It probably acted as a service tunnel for the water system. She had followed it and noticed a slippery path leading to the bottom. She had not ventured down it for fear of falling without some kind of support to hold onto. Obviously this was not going to be a deterrent for Tai Tek.

Reaching up, River climbed over the railing and ran to the open door. Pausing before entering, she waited a moment before doing a roll into the entrance way. To protect members of the House, they had been asked to remain in their living areas for the evening. Anyone outside the House would be considered hostile.

River came up beside a large plant near the door and took cover, looking around carefully. She could see a faint trail of blood leading through the foyer toward the stairs down to the training room. She smiled grimly. Tai Tek was on her home turf now. Just as she was about to move she heard footsteps running up the steps outside and four of Tai Tek's men ran in. Moving toward the stairs, River could see the panic on their faces as they looked wildly around as they ran.

"This was a suicide mission. No female is worth this!" one of the men growled as he ran. "Tai Tek was a fool to think he could defeat the House of Kassis. We are all dead men."

"Shut up. We have to get through the tunnel and down the mountain to the shuttle before he leaves us," another man growled.

River grinned. Yes, they were dead men if they got in her way. She would never have thought of herself as a bloodthirsty person, but these men had meant to kill her family. She could never let that happen.

River followed them quietly, stopping as she watched them turn around, trying to find their way in the maze of passages. They glanced at the floor, trying to follow the specks of blood Tai Tek had left. She was about to just kill them when an older man stepped out holding a laser pistol.

"Gentlemen, you are under arrest for your unauthorized entrance into the House of Kassis. Please drop your weapons, or I will be forced to eliminate you." Je'zi, the elderly man who had greeted them the first day, was standing, dressed in his uniform and holding a laser pistol.

River almost groaned. He looked like he was a hundred years old, and the pistol shook in his withered hand. The four large guards would have laughed if they hadn't been so desperate to escape.

"Move aside, old man," one of the men growled, pulling out a large sword.

"I'm afraid it is my duty..." Je'zi started to say.

The largest warrior growled and charged Je'zi. Je'zi fell as he moved backward into the room, pushing the door open. His laser charge hit the huge warrior in the shoulder before he slammed the door closed, knocking the male back a step. The warrior shook for a minute before transferring the sword to his other hand.

"Stop!" River called out, moving to stand behind the four men. She had four knives in her hand.

The men turned as one to look at River. "Please stand down. If you surrender and swear allegiance to the House of Kassis you have a chance to live. If not, you die now."

The men stared at the beautiful warrior woman standing in front of them. They had never seen anything like her before. She seemed to glow as she stood before them. Her hair hung down around her in waves, and her skirt and top clung to her, showcasing her willowy figure. Their eyes widened when they saw the knives she held in her hands.

"I will kill you before you even know you are dead. It is your choice," River said softly. "Tai Tek left you to die. You should have no loyalty to him."

The largest warrior snarled taking a step forward. "He promised us the females. I claim you!"

He took two steps toward River before freezing, a surprised look on his face. Grabbing at his neck, he felt the two knives embedded in it. River had already pulled two more knives to replace them.

"Does anyone else want to die?" River said coldly, looking on as the huge warrior collapsed on the floor in front of the others.

The three warriors looked at their dead companion and, quickly dropped their weapons.

Bending down on one knee, all three bowed their heads. "We pledge our allegiance to you, my lady."

"Je'zi, come out here," River called to the old man.

Je'zi opened the door to his room, cautiously peeking out. "Yes, Lady River?"

"Please see that these men are kept safe until my return. If they try to escape, kill them. I gave my word they will not be harmed unless they try to renege on their promise of allegiance. Am I clear?" River said loudly to make sure the old man heard her.

"Yes, Lady River. Keep them safe unless you need to kill them," Je'zi said.

River chuckled. "Close enough."

River looked at the men one more time before she nodded to them. Only when she felt sure they would no longer be a threat did she move quickly down the passage under the training room. She had one more threat to eliminate. This one was for Star.

Chapter 22

Torak slashed at the man who came at him out of the dark. He was prepared to kill anyone who got in his way. He moved quickly through the garden followed by a handful of his best men. His father and Gril Tal Mod were searching the South House for any remaining traitors.

Torak paused when he came upon the dead bodies at the main fountain. He knelt down, looking at the knives embedded in the two dead men. He looked up, trying to focus on the map in the lens. He saw River's identifying marker moving in their House, while Jo's and Star's remained in the garden. It was the last he saw before the lens disintegrated.

"Manota, Jazin, find Jo and Star. I will go after River. Kev, finish off anyone else in the garden." The men nodded grimly before separating.

* * *

Torak ran toward his House. The last he saw, River had been in the passageway near the Training room. He leaped up the steps into his House, pausing only briefly as he noticed a trail of blood. Panic hit him as he wondered if it was River's.

A dark, cold determination swept through him as he realized if River did not survive he would kill every man who ever thought to support Tai Tek before ending his own life. He knew with certainty he could never survive without her. Following the trail he came to the passageway where a huge warrior lay dead. Torak turned him over to see two knives protruding from his throat.

A door to his left opened slightly, and Je'zi peeked out. "Ah, my lord, Lady River went down below the training room to the passage containing the water system. She asked that I keep an eye on these gentlemen. She promised them safety if they pledged allegiance to your House, which they have. I am watching over them until her return."

Torak looked grimly at the three men sitting on the floor with their heads bowed. "Where is Tai Tek?"

One of the men looked up. "He goes through the passageway to a clearing on the other side of the river. A shuttle waits to carry him to a Tearnat starship."

"Who does he have with him?" Torak asked tersely.

"Just the female, Javonna. She is the one who told him about the passageway and modified the security system," the man said. "I pledge my allegiance, my lord, and my sword if you would allow it."

Torak looked at the young man for a moment before nodding. "I accept your pledge, but will decline your help this time."

The man nodded in understanding. He had never wanted to fight for Tai Tek, but the man had threatened to eliminate all of his family. He had no choice but to fight for him until he could secure their safety.

Torak turned and rushed down the passageway. He felt a sense of relief at the same time as burning anger ignited at River. She was carrying his son. How dare she pursue Tai Tek? He was going to tie her up and make sure she never put herself or their child in danger again. He turned the last corner and saw the door leading down into the cave wide open. Moving slower now, despite his desire to rush, he knew he could never protect his mate if he got himself killed.

* * *

River paused as she listened to Javonna's heavy panting. She crouched down, keeping as low as she could and still be able to move forward. She had caught up with Tai Tek and Javonna just as they were entering the passageway. The lock on the door had been blown apart by laser fire. The sound had given River the clue she needed to know how close Tai Tek had been. Now, she moved with caution. There was not a lot of room in the damp cave to move if he decided to fire his laser pistol. In addition, River knew Tai Tek's vision in the dark was superior to her own. Barely moving her head, she looked around the edge of a rock outcropping.

"Please, Tai Tek. Please, let me go," Javonna whined.

"Move it, bitch. I'm tired of your whining," Tai Tek said coldly, pulling Javonna behind him.

"No, you are just going to let your men have me. I won't survive that," Javonna cried out hoarsely. "You promised I could have Torak. You promised."

Tai Tek turned striking Javonna across the face, knocking her down. "You want that bastard Torak, you can have him."

Javonna screamed just as Tai Tek shot her with the laser pistol. "He can have your whining corpse."

River put her fist in her mouth as she stared at Javonna's unseeing eyes. She watched as Tai Tek turned to move toward the mouth of the cave. River followed, trying not to notice Javonna's blood seeping into the dirt floor of the cave. There was nothing she could do for the woman. She almost felt sorry for her. River moved slowly behind Tai Tek, knowing she would only have one chance to stop him.

River had been just about to step out into the center of the cave to get a good throw when two huge shadows appeared on either side of the cave. Two Tearnats moved to stand before Tai Tek.

"Where are the others?" one of the creatures hissed.

"They are dead. It was a trap. Torak, his father, and brothers knew about our attack. Gril Tal Mod and his mate helped," Tai Tek said coldly. "You were supposed to have taken care of them."

"They had left before we could kill them," the other creature hissed. "We must leave before we are discovered. We will have to regroup. The starship is ready."

Suddenly one of the creatures turned with a growl, looking into the cave. "I smell a female."

All three men turned to look down the cave where River stood pressed against the wall. River stood frozen for just a moment before she gasped in terror. One of the creatures moved with incredible speed toward her.

She didn't even think before throwing one knife after another. The creature growled before falling and sliding to a dead heap at her feet. River turned and took off running as fast as she could toward the door leading into the passageway.

A low growl followed her, and she could hear the thump of the other Tearnat behind her. Just as she felt the creature's hot breath on the back of her neck, she heard a yell for her to get down. Falling to the hard ground, River curled into a tight ball just as a blast from a laser pistol knocked the creature backward into the rock wall of the cave.

Torak's heart was in his throat as he heard the roar of the enraged Tearnat. He had broken into a run, moving in a blur through the tunnel. He saw River running back toward him just as a huge Tearnat was about to impale her with one of its long claws.

Yelling for River to get down, he fired his laser pistol on full charge at the creature, hitting him in the chest and knocking him back. The Tearnat's hard chest plate would protect him to some degree from the blast, but it at least got the creature away from River. Reaching down, Torak gripped River by the arm, swinging her up and behind him as the Tearnat shook off the blast.

"You are dead, Kassisan scum," the Tearnat growled as he pulled out his double-edged battle sword.

Torak threw the laser pistol to the side. The full charge combined with his previous use had drained it, and it was useless. Pulling his own sword he gripped the handle, charging the blade which glowed a bright blue.

The Tearnat swung his sword at Torak's head. Torak bent at the last second, slicing up and across the Tearnat's chest and opening a deep line over the hard breastplate. The Tearnat roared out in pain and surprise, moving a step back and touching his chest. A dark red stained its clawed hand.

"The blade on this can slice through anything, including your breastplate," Torak growled back.

The Tearnat hissed in fury at Torak. "I will kill you and mount your mate. She will die under me, Kassisan. I will enjoy fucking her and watching her scream as I tear her apart from the inside out."

Torak smiled cruelly. "Dead men don't fuck." With a turn, he sliced a deep cut across both of the Tearnat's thighs.

The Tearnat screamed out in rage as he swung his blade again. His blade cut a thin line across Torak's chest as Torak fell back. The blade continued until it struck the wall. Little bits of rock rained down on River and Torak as the creature pulled back his blade to strike at Torak again. Torak struck hard and fast, cutting deep wounds in the Tearnat's arm, then rolling to the side. The Tearnat was now bleeding from numerous cuts, some of them deep, but none of them fatal.

River worried about the cut on Torak's chest, watching as the front of his shirt turned red with blood. River bit down on her fist again as the Tearnat swung his sword at the same time as he kicked out one of his legs, striking Torak in the stomach and throwing him back against the rock wall. Torak grunted, barely bringing his own sword up in time to deflect the Tearnat's from ripping him in two.

River let out a cry as the Tearnat pinned Torak against the wall, pressing his blade closer to Torak's neck. Unable to stand the thought of losing Torak, River let loose a series of the crystal stars, lining the Tearnat's back from neck to waist with the sharp points.

The Tearnat reared back with a roar of pain turning toward River. River threw her two crystal hair pins just as Torak plunged his laser sword into the creature's belly. The Tearnat let out a strangled cry as he collapsed in a heap—the sword had gone straight through him, and River's two hair pins protruded from its throat.

"Oh Torak," River cried out, rushing toward him. She frantically pulled at his shirt, trying to see how bad the wound was.

Torak gripped River's hands tightly in his own, not wanting her to get his blood all over her. "Where is Tai Tek?"

"I saw him at the mouth of the cave," River replied, looking up into Torak's face trying to determine if he was all right. "Your chest..."

"It is just a flesh wound—nothing to worry about. Go back to our living quarters and lock yourself in," Torak said harshly. "I have to go after Tai Tek."

"No, you're hurt. If you go, so do I—" River started to argue.

Torak reached down and kissed River hard on the mouth before glaring down at her. "You promised to stay safe. You promised to protect yourself and our son."

River looked up at Torak, tears filling her eyes. "Star was hit. I don't know if she is alive. I promised to kill him."

Torak's look softened at the pain in River's eyes. Brushing her hair away from her face, he kissed her gently. He wanted to pull her into his arms, but he did not want his blood on her. It would be as if it were her blood. He couldn't stand to imagine how easily it could have been if Tai Tek had taken her.

"Come, but you must listen to me," Torak said. "Do you have any knives left?"

"Two," River replied softly.

Torak nodded. "Do not you endanger yourself or our son, do you understand? If I tell you to leave, you must."

River nodded silently. Torak looked down at River for a moment more before moving down the cave toward the rock ledge. Reaching the entrance they gazed down, watching as Tai Tek looked back briefly before climbing aboard a Tearnat shuttle.

Torak let out a curse. He spoke quickly into a com-link requesting the shuttle be intercepted and warning of a Tearnat starship in orbit. River watched as the shuttle turned, skimming the tall trees before disappearing over the mountains.

"Where do you think he is going?" River asked, never taking her eyes off the retreating shuttle.

"They probably have a base camp hidden in the Forbidden Region. It will be difficult to follow as the area is heavily covered in a mist that never dissipates," Torak said quietly, pulling River closer to his side. "Let us return to the others."

River looked up helplessly at Torak. "Torak, if Star—"

Torak shook his head, his fingers lying gently on River's lips. "She has been taken to medical. Jazin is with her."

River's lips trembled as the stress of what had happened that evening caught up with her. She buried her face in Torak's shoulder as a small sob escaped. She had never thought her life would turn out to be this way. She was fighting beside a man she loved on an alien planet. As River turned to look out over the river below, the twin moons casting diamonds on the water, she couldn't help the protective hand that covered her stomach.

She looked up startled when Torak covered her hand with his. "I love you, River. I do not think my heart can handle any more threats to you."

River gave Torak a watery smile. "Me either. Come, let's get you to medical. I want you healed so you can love me."

Chapter 23

River lay back on the bed watching as Torak dried his hair with a towel. The room was dark, even though the sun had risen hours ago, thanks to a simple command. They had returned to the South House to seek medical attention for Torak and to find out how Star was doing.

Ajaska and Gril Tal Mod had finished off Tai Tek's men who had not surrendered. Many of the men who had surrendered had sworn allegiance to the House of Kassis, stating they had only done what they had because Tai Tek held members of their families, many who were women and children, in a prison under his House threatening to kill them if they did not fight for him. Kev Mul Kar and his brother, Adron, Tai Tek's Captain of the Guard who had been working undercover for the Alliance, had left to search for and release the prisoners.

"I don't think I've ever seen Jazin so out of control," River said as she traced her finger over the thin sheet covering her.

"If Gril Tal Mod's mate had not gotten to Star when she did and taken her to medical, it would have been much worse," Torak said quietly, throwing the towel down on the end of the bed.

River let out a deep sigh as she stared at Torak's hard body. His chest was healed, and he did not even bother to wrap a towel around his waist when he came in from his shower. River had taken one an hour earlier while she waited for Torak to finish up with his father and brothers.

Tai Tek had escaped for now. Gril Tal Mod was furious to know that some of his people planned to kill not only him, but his mate. They were now working together to find the rebels who supported his late son's desire to continue the war. This confrontation created a stronger bond between the House of Kassis and the Clan of Tal Mod.

Star would remain in medical for a few more days as she had lost a lot of blood, and the healer thought it better to give Jazin more time to calm down. The last River heard from Jazin was "he was going to chain Star to his bed and never let her up again." She had chuckled as Star rolled her eyes weakly before falling asleep on him.

River reached for Torak as he climbed into the bed next to her. She smiled as he pulled her tight against his body. "You know I have to punish you for disobeying me, don't you?" he murmured as he began kissing her neck.

"Punish me?" River moaned. "I hope it includes ropes and clamps and... Oh yes, baby," River breathed out as Torak moved over River clamping down on her nipple and pushing her thighs apart.

"You are lucky you are with child. Otherwise, I think a flogging would have been in order or at least a spanking you would never forget," Torak murmured huskily.

River moaned again as the picture of Torak spanking her flashed through her mind. "You can do it if you are gentle," she murmured against his mouth.

Torak moved between River's thighs, pushing his swollen cock against her slick entrance. "Not yet. Right now I want to love you slowly," he whispered against her lips as he filled her. "I need to see your beautiful face as I make love to you knowing you are safe in my arms."

River moaned as he pushed his thick length into her. She ran her fingers through his hair, loving the feel of the silky texture. "I love you so much, Torak."

Torak crushed River's lips to his, drinking her as he began moving, slowly at first, then more aggressively as his need to claim her took over him. Never again did he want to experience the fear of losing River. As he kissed her shoulder, her neck, her face, and her lips, he felt his climax building to a level he had never experienced before, as if all his love for her was about to explode from him.

He cried out as River clamped down on him, her own climax breaking over her in powerful waves of ecstasy. His body jerked as he released the last of his seed deep into her womb. At the thought of how close he had come to once again losing River and their unborn son, his shoulders began to shake.

River ran her hands over Torak's shoulders and down his back, feeling a hot dampness on her neck. "Torak, what's wrong? Are you hurt?" River asked anxiously, stroking him.

Torak leaned back before rolling over and pulling River on top of him. "I can never lose you, River." His hand moved down to her stomach and lay there gently. "You are my mate and the mother of my son. I cannot stand the thought of the danger you were in this past night. It could easily have been you who had been hurt... killed," he whispered.

"But, I wasn't. You saved me," River said, giving Torak a kiss. "You are my protector, my mate, and the father of my son. Together we will protect him. As long as we are together, we are stronger."

"Together, forever," Torak said with a smile before rolling over and kissing River.

"Now, I think I am ready to give you your punishment," Torak said with a sexy grin.

River's giggle turned to a moan as she moved beneath Torak's growing length. "I'm looking forward to it. Now, about those ropes..." she murmured.

To be continued:
Star's Journey: Lords of Kassis Book 2

Preview of *Star's Storm*

(Lords of Kassis: Book 2)

Synopsis

Star Strauss has always been a fighter. From the time she was born prematurely to her life on the road as a circus performer. She has never let her small stature keep her from achieving her dreams. She is one of the best aerial performers in the world. Her love of being up high and flying free has helped her overcome the challenges she faces when she is on the ground. Only her circus family, her sister, and her best friend have ever really understood her need for freedom. Her life changes when she finds herself on a distant world where every creature seems to tower over her.

Jazin Ja Kel Coradon is the third son of the ruling House of Kassis. He is known not only for his skills as a fierce warrior, but for his knowledge of communication, security, and weapons systems. This knowledge has increased the effectiveness of the Kassis defenses protecting their world from attack from a new group of rebels who threaten their very existence. He will fight until his last breath to protect his people.

His life changes when he meets a tiny creature who is unlike anything he has ever seen. She is petite, delicate, and beautiful. The problem is she is also the strongest, most stubborn female he has ever met. She refuses to do what he tells her, she defies him at every turn, and doesn't seem to understand that all he wants to do is protect her. If he could just get her to stay in the nice safe bubble he has created for her, his life would be so much simpler!

Star had enough of people back home trying to put her in a glass box, she wasn't about to let anyone on an alien world try to put her in one! When the man she loves is kidnapped, she will do what she does best. She will use her skills as a performer to rescue him from the men determined to extract the information they need to bring down the Kassis defense system before they kill him.

Sometimes being small has its advantages. The enemy never expects a pint-size female to have the strength of a warrior and a stubborn warrior is about to find out he has a partner who can stand tall with him in the face of danger.

If you loved this story by me (S.E. Smith) please leave a review. You can also take a look at additional books and sign up for my newsletter at **http://sesmithfl.com** to hear about my latest releases or keep in touch using the following links:

Website: http://sesmithfl.com
Newsletter: http://sesmithfl.com/?s=newsletter
Facebook: https://www.facebook.com/se.smith.5
Twitter: https://twitter.com/sesmithfl
Pinterest: http://www.pinterest.com/sesmithfl/
Blog: http://sesmithfl.com/blog/
Forum: http://www.sesmithromance.com/forum/

Excerpts of S.E. Smith Books

If you would like to read more S.E. Smith stories, she recommends Hunter's Claim, the first in her Alliance series. Or if you prefer a Paranormal or Western with a twist, you can check out Lily's Cowboys or Indiana Wild...

Additional Books by S.E. Smith

Short Stories and Novellas
For the Love of Tia
    (Dragon Lords of Valdier Book 4.1)
A Dragonling's Easter
    (Dragonlings of Valdier Book 1.1)
A Dragonling's Haunted Halloween
    (Dragonlings of Valdier Book 1.2)

A Dragonling's Magical Christmas
    (Dragonlings of Valdier Book 1.3)
A Warrior's Heart
    (Marastin Dow Warriors Book 1.1)
Rescuing Mattie
    (Lords of Kassis: Book 3.1)

Science Fiction/Paranormal Novels

Cosmos' Gateway Series

Tink's Neverland (Cosmos' Gateway: Book 1)
Hannah's Warrior (Cosmos' Gateway: Book 2)
Tansy's Titan (Cosmos' Gateway: Book 3)
Cosmos' Promise (Cosmos' Gateway: Book 4)
Merrick's Maiden (Cosmos' Gateway Book 5)

Curizan Warrior

Ha'ven's Song (Curizan Warrior: Book 1)

Dragon Lords of Valdier

Abducting Abby (Dragon Lords of Valdier: Book 1)
Capturing Cara (Dragon Lords of Valdier: Book 2)
Tracking Trisha (Dragon Lords of Valdier: Book 3)
Ambushing Ariel (Dragon Lords of Valdier: Book 4)
Cornering Carmen (Dragon Lords of Valdier: Book 5)
Paul's Pursuit (Dragon Lords of Valdier: Book 6)
Twin Dragons (Dragon Lords of Valdier: Book 7)

Lords of Kassis Series

River's Run (Lords of Kassis: Book 1)
Star's Storm (Lords of Kassis: Book 2)
Jo's Journey (Lords of Kassis: Book 3)
Ristéard's Unwilling Empress (Lords of Kassis: Book 4)

Magic, New Mexico Series

Touch of Frost (Magic, New Mexico Book 1)
Taking on Tory (Magic, New Mexico Book 2)

Sarafin Warriors

Choosing Riley (Sarafin Warriors: Book 1)

Viper's Defiant Mate (Sarafin Warriors Book 2)
The Alliance Series
Hunter's Claim (The Alliance: Book 1)
Razor's Traitorous Heart (The Alliance: Book 2)
Dagger's Hope (The Alliance: Book 3)
Zion Warriors Series
Gracie's Touch (Zion Warriors: Book 1)
Krac's Firebrand (Zion Warriors: Book 2)

Paranormal and Time Travel Novels
Spirit Pass Series
Indiana Wild (Spirit Pass: Book 1)
Spirit Warrior (Spirit Pass Book 2)
Second Chance Series
Lily's Cowboys (Second Chance: Book 1)
Touching Rune (Second Chance: Book 2)

Young Adult Novels
Breaking Free Series
Voyage of the Defiance (Breaking Free: Book 1)

Recommended Reading Order Lists:
http://sesmithfl.com/reading-list-by-events/
http://sesmithfl.com/reading-list-by-series/

About S.E. Smith

S.E. Smith is a *New York Times,* **USA TODAY,** *International, and Award-Winning* Bestselling author of science fiction, fantasy, paranormal, and contemporary works for adults, young adults, and children. She enjoys writing a wide variety of genres that pull her readers into worlds that take them away.

CPSIA information can be obtained
at www.ICGtesting.com
Printed in the USA
FFHW02n0249011018
48576778-52485FF